THE SANTINA CROWN

Royalty has never been so scandalous!

STOP THE PRESS—*Crown prince in shock marriage*

The tabloid headlines…

When Crown Prince Alessandro of Santina proposes to paparazzi favorite Allegra Jackson it promises to be the social event of the decade—outrageous headlines guaranteed!

The salacious gossip…

Harlequin Presents invites you to rub shoulders with royalty, sheikhs and glamorous socialites. Step into the decadent playground of the world's rich and famous, where **one thing is for sure—royalty has never been so scandalous!**

Each month enjoy a new installment from The Santina Crown miniseries,

beginning May 2012!

THE PRICE OF ROYAL DUTY—Penny Jordan

THE SHEIKH'S HEIR—Sharon Kendrick

SANTINA'S SCANDALOUS PRINCESS—Kate Hewitt

THE MAN BEHIND THE SCARS—Caitlin Crews

DEFYING THE PRINCE—Sarah Morgan

PRINCESS FROM THE SHADOWS—Maisey Yates

THE GIRL NOBODY WANTED—Lynn Raye Harris

PLAYING THE ROYAL GAME—Carol Marinelli

Collect all 8 volumes!

"Don't you think you're being a tad dramatic?" he asked her in a wry voice.

'I'm not being dramatic," she defended herself. "Surely I should have some rights as a person, a human being, some say in my own fate, instead of having my future decided for me by my father. To endure marriage to a man who has agreed to marry me simply because he wants an heir, and to whom my father has virtually auctioned me off in exchange for a royal alliance."

"I should have thought such a marriage would suit you, Sophia. After all, it's well documented that your own chosen lifestyle involves something very similar, when it comes to bed-hopping."

A body blow indeed, and one that drove the blood from Sophia's face and doubled the pain in her heart. It shouldn't matter what Ash thought of her. That was not part of her plan. But still, his denunciation of her hurt and it wasn't one she could defend herself against. Not without telling him far more than she wanted him to know.

"Then you thought wrong" was all she could permit herself to say. "That is not the kind of marriage I want. I can't bear the thought of this marriage." Her panic and fear was there in her voice; even she could hear it, so how much more obvious must it be to Ash?

She must try to stay calm. Not even to Ash could she truly explain the distaste, the loathing, the fear she had of being forced by law to give herself in a marriage bed in the most intimate way possible when… No, that was one secret that she must keep no matter what, just as she had already kept it for so long.

"Please, Ash, I'm begging you for your help."

Penny Jordan

THE PRICE OF ROYAL DUTY

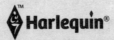

TORONTO NEW YORK LONDON
AMSTERDAM PARIS SYDNEY HAMBURG
STOCKHOLM ATHENS TOKYO MILAN MADRID
PRAGUE WARSAW BUDAPEST AUCKLAND

ISBN-13: 978-0-373-13066-5

Recycling programs for this product may not exist in your area.

THE PRICE OF ROYAL DUTY

First North American Publication 2012

Copyright © 2012 by Harlequin Books S.A.

Special thanks and acknowledgment are given to Penny Jordan for her contribution to *The Santina Crown* series.

www.Harlequin.com

Printed in U.S.A.

All about the author...
Penny Jordan

PENNY JORDAN has been writing for more than twenty-five years and has an outstanding record—more than 165 novels published, including the phenomenally successful *A Perfect Family, To Love, Honor and Betray, The Perfect Sinner* and *Power Play*, which hit the *Sunday Times* and *New York Times* bestseller lists. She says she hopes to go on writing until she has passed the 200 mark—and maybe even the 250 mark.

Although Penny was born in Preston, Lancashire, where she spent her childhood, she moved to Cheshire as a teenager, and has continued to live there. Following the death of her husband she moved to the small traditional Cheshire market town on which she based her Crighton books.

She lives with her Birman cat Posh, who tries to assist with her writing by sitting on the newspapers and magazines Penny reads to provide her with ideas she can adapt for her fiction.

Penny is a member and supporter of the Romantic Novelists' Association and the Romance Writers of America—two organizations dedicated to providing support for both published and yet-to-be-published authors.

Other titles by Penny Jordan available in ebook:

Harlequin Presents®

*Russian Rivals

CHAPTER ONE

'*Ash.*' Sophia Santina, youngest daughter of the King and Queen of the island of Santina, breathed the name silently to herself, almost reverentially. Just the feel of the nearly silent breath that whispered his name and caressed her throat was enough to raise erotic pinpricks of desire within her flesh. Ash. How the whispering of his name was enough to unleash within her an aching echo of the tumultuous teenage desires he had once aroused in her. The very air was electric with the reckless sensual excitement that wantonly flooded her, even though she had sworn she would not, positively not, allow herself to experience it.

She had known, of course, that he had been invited to her eldest brother's engagement party here at the castle that was their family home, but knowing that and actually seeing him with that strikingly sensual maleness of his that she remembered so well were two very different things.

She would have recognised him anywhere, just as she had done now merely from her brief glimpse of the back view of him as he walked into the ballroom and then turned to refuse a glass of champagne. Just the turn of his head, just the thick dark sheen of his hair and the way it curled into the nape of his neck, was enough to conjure up old memories. Memories of longing recklessly for the right to bury her fingers in its softness, curl them around its strands and then urge his mouth down to her own. A shudder of sensual awareness jolted through her. Some things never changed. A certain kind of need, a certain kind of desire, a certain kind of love.

First love? Surely only a fool believed that first love was an only love, and she prided herself on not being that. No, Ash had killed that tremulous, tender love when he had rejected her, telling her that she was a child still who was putting herself in danger by offering herself to a man of his age, that she was fortunate that his own sense of honour and the repugnance he felt at the very thought of taking what she offered meant that she was protected from him taking advantage of her naivety. Telling her that even if she had been older he would not have wanted her because he was wholly committed to someone else.

She had promised herself then that in future her love would only be given to a man who was worthy of it and who valued it and her. A man who loved her as much as she did him. And because of that promise to herself, she needed Ash's help now, no matter how much her pride reacted angrily against that need.

Putting down her virtually untouched drink, she started to walk towards him.

Standing in the packed ballroom in the castle on the Mediterranean island of Santina, the official residence and home of the royal family of Santina, Ashok Achari, Maharaja of Nailpur, frowned as his grim, obsidian gaze swept the scene in front of him. Beyond the open doors to the stunningly elegant ballroom with its crystal chandeliers and antique mirrors stood footmen wearing the livery of the royal family. An impressive dress-uniformed group of the king's own personal guard had been standing motionless in front of the castle in honour of the occasion and the guests. As a fellow royal, Ash had seen them salute him as the limousine that had picked him up from the airport had swept up to the main entrance. It was plain that no expense was being spared to celebrate the engagement of the king's eldest son and heir.

His fellow guests milled around him, and laughter and the sound of conversation filled the air.

Ash had gone to school with the groom-to-be, Alex, and they were still close friends. Even so, he hadn't wanted to attend this engagement party as he had more pressing matters to deal with at home, but duty was important to Ash—far more so than any personal desires—and duty had compelled him to accept.

He had, though, ordered his pilot to have his private jet standing ready to fly him back to Mumbai where he had an important business meeting in the morning.

A sixth sense had him turning round just as an exquisitely beautiful petite brunette came hurrying towards him.

Sophia.

A woman now, not the girl she had been the last time he had seen her in person. Where he had remembered a girl trembling on the brink of womanhood, innocent and eager, in need of protection from herself, he was now being confronted by a woman who clearly knew all about her sexuality and its power and how to both use it and take pleasure from it. That his body had recorded and registered that information in the time it had taken him to exhale and breathe again pointed to a weakness within himself of which he had previously been unaware.

The shock of his instant male awareness of Sophia as a woman had caught him totally off guard and Ash did not like that. That kind of thing was not something he permitted himself to do. It smacked too much of a hidden repressed need and Ash did not allow himself to have hidden repressed needs—needs that could make him vulnerable. Besides, the very idea of him being vulnerable to Sophia was laughable. She wasn't his type. No? So why then was his body reacting to her as though it had never seen a woman before?

A momentary lapse. He was a man, she was a woman, and his bed had been empty since he had dismissed his last mistress. If he was aroused by the sight of Sophia then it was probably completely natural. After all, from the luxuriant tumble of long, dark brown waves via the stunning beauty of her delicately shaped face with its dark eyes and soft full lips to the voluptuous curves of her sensationally sensually shaped body, Sophia Santina was an instant, irresistible magnet for male attention—and his own body was reacting just like any other heterosexual man's would. Wasn't it?

Yes. He would be a fool if he allowed that reaction more importance than it merited. To be caught off guard by a surge of physical desire so strong that he was glad of the packed floor of the ballroom and the darkness of his dinner suit to conceal the evidence of his reaction to her was an alien experience for him and added aggravation to what he was already experiencing. He had no desire whatsoever to be aroused by any woman right now, never mind Sophia Santina.

But he couldn't deny the fact that he was. Not with that arousal already straining at the expensive fabric of his suit, despite the ferocity of the mental control with which he was attempting to prevent it.

She was still coming towards him and in another handful of seconds she would be flinging herself into his arms, just as she had done as a young girl. And if she did that... His body beat out a raw demanding pulsing clarion call of lust. Ash cursed inwardly. He was a man who prided himself on his control of his appetites, especially when it came to sex.

It meant nothing that Sophia was sexually desirable and—if one believed the gossip press—sexually available, as well, should a man chance to catch her attention. Desiring her wasn't on his agenda for where he planned to take his life and it never would be.

Apart from anything else, as he had already reminded himself, Sophia simply wasn't his type. Following the death of his wife, the women with whom he had shared his bed had all been elegant long-limbed women skilled in the arts of sexual pleasure, with cool logical minds in whose lives emotions did not play a part. Women who, when the game ended, gracefully accepted the generous gift he gave them and left his bed as discreetly as they had entered it.

Sophia was not like that. Sophia, as he well knew from watching her grow up, was an intense melding of passionate emotions. A man who took her to bed would need... His body reacted again, causing him to have to shift his weight from one leg to the other in an attempt to ensure that that reaction was disguised. There was no question of him taking Sophia to his bed. Not now, not ever.

'Ash,' Sophia said again, automatically stepping forward to embrace him, her eyes widening when he immediately encircled her wrist with his right hand to fend her off while stepping back from her in rejection.

How could she have been so stupid? There was, after all, a history of rejection between them, or rather of Ash rejecting her, and now she had put herself on the back foot by allowing him to feel that he needed to push her away. In her anxiety to plead for his help she had acted foolishly. She must be more mentally alert, she warned herself.

Yes, an inner voice argued defensively, but all she had been doing was greeting him as she would greet anyone she knew well, not coming on to him. She opened her mouth ready to make a feisty protest and berate him for misinterpreting her gesture and then closed it again, as she controlled her emotions. This was not the time to antagonise him, no matter how strongly she felt that she was being misjudged. And now that she was so close to him, she could see what she hadn't seen before: the change in him that was clearly written in the steely uncompromising coldness of his expression.

Against her will, sadness locked her throat. The Ash she remembered had been a warm, outgoing young man who had laughed a lot and enjoyed life. What had happened to change him and turn him into the cynical, almost-brooding man in front of her now? Did she really need to ask herself that? He had lost his wife, a wife whom he had loved.

Her sadness grew, compassion for the Ash she remembered filling her. That Ash had been a young man whose innate kindness—especially to the young sister of a school friend on those holiday visits he had made to the island—had made that girl feel for the first time in her life that someone understood her, and valued her. His kindness and his understanding had meant so much to her, and it was her memory of those things that had brought her to his side now and not the abrupt sea change in their relationship as she had turned from a girl to a woman, and his rejection of her because of it.

Those qualities though had been stripped from the man in front of her now, Sophia recognised with a sudden painful jolt of her heart into her ribs. This Ash possessed a dark and brooding air that she didn't remember, along with a cold remoteness, as though somehow a dark cloud had darkened the warmth of the personality of the young man she remembered.

Something deep within her ached for what he had been. Immediately, Sophia clamped down on that feeling. She must not allow herself to be vulnerable to him emotionally. She must not feel anything for him. Not even when she had once patterned her ideal of what she thought desirable in a man on Ash himself? That had been a foolish mistake and one for which she had paid through the heartbreak that only the young and idealistic can know. The reality was that right now she should be feeling glad that he had changed and that there was therefore no danger of her being foolish enough to...

To what? To still feel something for him?

That was impossible.

But what if her responsiveness to him both physically and emotionally was burned into her DNA? *Burned into it?* Sophia winced. *Burned* was the correct word and she still had the scars to prove that. But those scars protected her now. She would never make the same mistake again. She was immune to Ash now and she intended to remain immune. She wasn't sixteen any more, after all.

Before, she had been filled with a young, romantic teenager's need to taste the apple the serpent had offered to Eve, and she had turned to Ash to help her assuage that need. That had been a terrible mistake for which she had paid in tears of shame and anguish.

Now she had to think past that, to that innocent time when she had merely seen Ash as her saviour, the one person she could turn to, to help her, the person who had, after all, saved her very life on more than one occasion. It was that Ash she desperately wanted to talk to right now, the words she would use to elicit the help she needed from him honed and practised. Now though she was beginning to recognise that somehow she couldn't just simply turn back and open the gate into the garden of innocence whose pathways Ash had walked with her when she had been a child.

She must not give up hope. She could not, Sophia reminded herself. But she must be careful. Careful and aware of what she needed to achieve for her own survival. This was just one meeting. One ordeal she had to go through to gain something she desperately needed. After tonight she would never have to see Ash again and she would be safe, from her own past and from the future her father planned for her.

She took a deep breath, and informed him with cool self-control, 'You can let go of me now, Ash. I promise you I won't touch you.'

Not touch him. Little did she know that his body, his flesh, his manhood, was screaming out to be touched by her. Inside his head, to his own self-disgust and anger, Ash could all too easily mentally visualise— right here, right now, in this packed and very public place—the need his flesh felt for him to place her hand over the hard aching pulse of his sex. No wonder she had the reputation she did if this was the effect she could have on his body. On his body, but not on him. That could not be permitted. Abruptly he released her wrist.

The very speed with which Ash released her proved to Sophia what her heart had already told her, namely that as far as he was concerned any physical contact between them was as taboo now as it had been when she had been sixteen.

And yet, as she had just reminded herself, Ash had once been kind to her. Very kind, indeed. The truth was that he had been her hero, her one place of safety and comfort.

Perhaps that was why, despite the dismissal and that brooding air of withdrawal about him, somehow, instinctively, if foolishly, she still felt as though Ash was the one person in her world to whom she could turn for help, should she need it. Or perhaps it was because she was desperate and there was no one else. And right now she certainly needed help. And needed it very much, indeed.

However, his grim manner had put a barrier between them so that now she was forced to recognise how misplaced her confidence in his kindness had been. And how much the change she could see in him complicated a plan which had seemed so simple when she had lain alone in her bed helplessly searching for a way to escape her fate.

She could easily have told the old Ash, the Ash she

remembered, what the problem was and just as easily have begged him to play the role she needed him to for the course of this evening. But this Ash, who looked at her with a gaze that held no affection for their shared past, but which instead seemed to look broodingly into a past that excluded her, diminished the hope she had brought with her to tonight's party.

But he *had* helped her in the past, she reminded herself. And not just helped her. He had saved her from death—not just once but twice. As she needed him to save her again now from another kind of death. The death that came from being sacrificed in a marriage to a man she had never met but whose reputation told her that he was everything she could never want in a husband.

Somehow she must find a way of breaking through the barriers between them, because without Ash's understanding, without his aid, her plan simply could not succeed.

And if he rejected her—again?

She must not think of that. She must be honest with him. She must beg him for his help. Taking another deep breath, she began, 'Ash, there's something I want to ask you.'

'If it's which of your current string of young men you should take to your bed next then I'm afraid I don't give that kind of advice. And anyway, you seem very skilled at picking the one that will gain you the most print inches and the largest photographs in the world's celebrity press.'

It was an emotionally brutal rebuttal and rejection, and that hurt. She knew she had her detractors but somehow she had not been prepared for Ash to be one of them. Because she wanted him to remember her as the innocent girl he had protected?

What if she did? It was only because she needed him to remember that relationship. As for that sharp stinging pain his words had brought her, that was nothing. She was not going to allow it any power. Even so, she couldn't stop herself from defending her actions. 'So I go public with my...relationships and you keep yours private.' She gave a small shrug, intending it to be dismissive.

'Which of us, I wonder, would an unbiased bystander consider to be the more honest?'

She had her own reasons for not just allowing but positively encouraging the world at large to think of her as a young woman who relished her hedonistically sexual lifestyle and who indeed revelled in it. After all, wasn't the best way to disguise and protect something precious to camouflage it, to hide it from view in plain sight?

Sophia daring to call his morals into question was something Ash's pride could not tolerate, especially when... Especially when, what? Especially when he had once taken on the responsibility of protecting her from the consequences of her emerging sexual needs because of those morals? Or especially when he was already having to deal with the private fallout he was facing inside himself from his still-active, and very much unwanted, physical sexual reaction to her?

His voice as hard and unforgiving as his expression, he told her curtly, 'But I'm afraid that such discussions aren't of any appeal to me, Sophia, no matter how much idle chatter and currency they might find amongst your friends. Now if you'll excuse me, I must go and thank your parents for this evening, as I have to be back in Mumbai tomorrow morning, and I'm flying out just after midnight.'

He was leaving so soon? That was something else she hadn't expected or prepared herself for. The window of opportunity that was her planned escape was closing down by the minute. Panic had started to build up inside her, a panic that had her blurting out emotionally, 'Ash, once you were different, kinder. Kind to me…my saviour… You saved my life.' Only desperation could be making her behave like this, betray herself like this. 'I know from the charities in which you are involved and the help you give to your people how philanthropic and good you are to those in need. Right now, Ash, I need…' She stopped, her breath locking in her throat. 'I've never been able to say to you how sorry I was about the death of your wife. I know how much she and your marriage meant to you.'

He was withdrawing from her, she could sense it, almost feel it in the chilling of the air between them. She had learned young how to judge other people's emotions and to be wary of antagonising them. She shouldn't have mentioned his late wife. So why had she? No reason. She had just wanted…

There was a flicker of something in those dark eyes, a tightening of the flesh that clung with such powerful sensuality to the bone structure of regal facial features with a lineage that went back across the centuries to a time when his warrior ancestors had roamed and ruled the desert plains of India. She knew she had angered him.

He was angry with her. For what? Mentioning his wife? Sophia knew how much he had loved the Indian princess he had married but it was several years now since her death and she was sure his bed hadn't remained empty during those years. Bedding someone was one thing, but as Sophia knew, loving them was another thing entirely.

However, if he thought he was going to frighten her off with his forbidding manner towards her, he was wrong. He no doubt remembered her as the young girl who was very easily hurt by any hint that she might have offended the man she hero-worshipped so intensely, but she wasn't that young girl any more, and when it came to being hurt and surviving that hurt… well, she could easily lay claim to having qualified for a master's degree in that particular emotional journey.

Ash could feel the tension invading his body. Sophia had dared to mention his marriage. He allowed no one to do that. It was a taboo subject.

'I do not discuss either my late wife or our marriage with anyone.'

The words delivered in a harsh blistering tone only confirmed what Sophia already felt she knew, and that was how much Ash still loved his dead wife.

She must not think about that, though. She must think instead about her own need for his help.

From the minute she had learned he was coming to the engagement party, she had seen him as her salvation and her only hope of rescue from a situation she simply could not bear. She must not falter now, no matter how vulnerable she felt inside.

Sophia had gone silent. Ash turned to look at her. She was trying to appear confident but he could see the apprehension beneath. It was a protective device she had often employed as a child. A child who as the youngest of the family, and a girl, was often overlooked. Somehow against his will, he found his anger receding.

Ash's penetrating gaze was assessing her with hawklike scrutiny, Sophia recognised, and yet there was something in his expression that had softened, as though the bones of his face had subtly moved so that she could see again the Ash whose memory she cherished, beneath the harshness that time had overlaid on those bones—something that resurrected her desperate hope.

There was no time to waste, she decided. She must be brave and strong, and trust in her own judgement, her own belief in him.

'My father wants to marry me to off to some Spanish prince he's found.'

What was that sensation that uncurled inside him and attacked with the deadly speed of a poisonous snake, causing his heart to lurch inside his chest? Nothing. Nothing at all.

'So your father wishes to arrange a dynastic and diplomatic marriage for you.'

Ash shrugged dismissively, but Sophia stopped him. 'It would be a forced marriage, and I would be the one forced into it.'

Her words might have been those of the passionate, emotional, sensitive young girl he remembered. How fierce she had been then in her defence of people's personal freedoms, her conviction that everyone had the right to dictate the pathway of their own lives. It was no real wonder given how often she and her father had clashed, as they were obviously doing now.

'Don't you think you're being a tad dramatic?' he asked her in a wry voice. 'You aren't a naive girl any more, Sophia. Royalty marries royalty, that is the way of our kind. Marriages are arranged, heirs conceived and born, and that is how we fulfil our duty to our fore-bears and our people.'

This was not how she had imagined he would react when she had lain sleepless at night, longing for his arrival, aching for his help, needing his support.

'I'm not being dramatic,' she defended herself. 'Surely I should have some rights as a person, a human being, some say in my own fate, instead of having my future decided for me by my father?'

'I'm sure he only has your best interests at heart.'

Ash just did not want to get involved in this. Why should he? He was a busy man about to enter the final negotiations on a contract, the success of which would secure the future of his people for generations to come.

'No. No,' she denied immediately. 'He doesn't have my best interests at heart. All he is interested in is se-curing a royal marriage for a daughter of the house of Santina. He told me that himself when I begged him to reconsider, that he had had to promise this Spanish prince that I would be an obedient and dutiful wife, a wife who would not try to interfere in his own preferred lifestyle of bed hopping amongst his many mistresses.

'When I told him that I didn't want to marry this prince, he said that I was ungrateful and ignoring my royal duty. He said that I would grow accustomed to my husband. Accustomed. To endure marriage to a man who has simply agreed to marry me because he wants an heir, and to whom my father has virtually auctioned me off in exchange for a royal alliance. How could that ever be having my best interests at heart?'

'I should have thought such a marriage would suit

you, Sophia. After all, it's well documented that your own chosen lifestyle involves something very similar, when it comes to bed hopping.'

A body blow indeed and one that drove the blood from Sophia's face and doubled the pain in her heart. It shouldn't matter what Ash thought of her. That was not part of her plan. But still his denunciation of her hurt and it wasn't one she could defend herself against. Not without telling him far more than she wanted him to know.

'Then you thought wrong,' was all she could permit herself to say. 'That is not the kind of marriage I want. I can't bear the thought of this marriage.' Her panic and fear was there in her voice; even she could hear it herself, so how much more obvious must it be to Ash?

She must try to stay calm. Not even to Ash could she truly explain the distaste, the loathing, the fear, she had of being forced by law to give herself in a marriage bed in the most intimate way possible when… No, that was one secret that she must keep no matter what, just as she had already kept it for so long.

Not even to Ash? Definitely not to Ash. Now she *was* letting her emotions get muddled instead of focusing on the practicalities of her situation.

Steadying her breathing she told Ash as calmly as she could, 'When I marry I want to know and respect my husband and our marriage. I want to love him and be loved by him. I want us to bring our children up in the safe secure circle of that love.' That, after all, was the truth.

And it was a truth that Ash heard and couldn't refute. He frowned. Against his will he was forced to acknowledge that there was something in her voice that touched old nerves, revived old memories. Revived them? Since when had they really needed reviving? He had never forgotten, could never forget.

'Please, Ash, I'm begging you for your help.'

CHAPTER TWO

THOSE words—the same words with which she had cried out to him once before—sliced through his self-control, cutting the cords that held fast the doors to the past.

Once before Sophia had begged him for something.

She'd been just past her sixteenth birthday the last time he'd seen her. He could still remember the shock he had felt at seeing her all grown-up. One minute—or so it had seemed—she had been a child, but somehow six months later she had been trembling on the brink of what would become her womanhood, a girl still for all her burgeoning physical maturity, a girl with tears tracking down her cheeks, her huge dark brown eyes drowning in tears. Then she had still been an innocent: naive, unknowing, virginal and vulnerable. He had been determined that it would not be through him that any of those things were taken from her, no matter how hard she begged him to do so.

What had happened to her during those intervening years to turn her into the wanton sensualist she was now? Why should he care? The sixteen-year-old towards whom he had felt so protective belonged to another life, another Ash.

Even then she'd been sensationally beautiful, with

everything about her already hinting at the sensuality to come. Then she had had the promise of a sweet, almost ready-to-ripen peach, yet still a girl compared to his adult-male maturity, and his natural sense of responsibility and moral probity had naturally reacted to that. He had known that he had a duty towards her to protect her not just from herself but from that shock of awareness within himself of the fact that she was becoming a desirable woman.

Ash discovered that there was suddenly a sour taste in his mouth. For himself. For that brief ripping through his moral code, caused by the shocking sexual awareness he'd had of her when he had seen the change in her. Desires he never should have had for that girl given the protective role he had previously played in her life and the fact that he had been about to be married.

Desires he still had for her? He swallowed hard against that question. She was a woman, and available. He was a man, but he could not allow himself to want her. He *would* not allow it. After all, he had nothing left within him to give to a woman like Sophia, who so obviously brought emotional passion to her relationships along with her sexual desire. A grim wryness filled him. So he was back in his old role towards her, was he, protecting her from his own desire?

'Ash, please.' The panic in Sophia's voice made Ash frown. Twice before he had heard her say his name in that same tone of mingled fear and need and now somehow his body reacted to that memory, instinctively halting him in his tracks.

'Sophia...'

'Please, Ash. I need you. There isn't anyone else I can turn to.'

'No? What about one of those young men who share your bed?' His challenge was harsh and acerbic.

This was getting dangerous, Sophia recognised. The conversation was going now in a direction she most certainly did not want.

'That's just sex. What I need from you is help.'

Just sex? Ash could almost taste the ferocity of the atavistic emotions surging through him.

Across the years that separated him from those other occasions inside his head he could see the sixteen-year-old she had been, pleading with him for something it was impossible for him to give her. He could almost smell the hot summer fragrance of the small grassy bank on which they'd been sitting. Inside his head he could see a clear image of her in her thin cotton dress. It had shown quite clearly the perfect shape of her high rounded breasts with their eager thrusting nipples pushing against the fabric, just as she had pushed against his chest with small fists when she had begged him to take her and show her what it was to be a woman—and the icy cold shock to his system it had given him to realise that his awareness of her was darkened by the sexual desire. He had wanted to walk away from her there and then, to put an end to the danger he could sense, but before he could do anything she had continued emotionally, 'I'm the only girl in my class who's still a virgin, and I hate it. The other girls laugh at me because of it. They say that I'm a baby and…'

He could still remember the duality of the feelings her confession had brought him. Firstly, a desire to protect her and defend her, but beneath that, shockingly and shamefully, a slow awareness of the sweet pleasure there would be for the man to whom she would ultimately give herself for the first time. He had reminded himself that he was too old for her, and that she was too young for him. To even think about doing as she asked would be an abuse of their relationship that could never be allowed, but still there had been, inside his head, that treacherous thought that were she two years or so older and he two years or more younger… He would what? Bed her and then leave her—dishonour her—for the marriage that had been arranged for him since childhood? Never.

And so he had put temptation aside and told her as though it was no concern to him, 'I'm sure there are any number of boys your own age who would be delighted to relieve you of your virginity.'

'I don't want it to be them, I want it to be you,' she insisted, her eyes dark and stormy with the heat of her need.

Only he knew how tempted he'd been to wish away some of the years that separated them and to give in and take her. Just the smell of her sun-warmed skin had sent him half maddened with aching, longing to lie her down and lick and kiss his way over every inch of her delectable, hotly eager body until he reached those dark flaunting nipples. Inside his head he had already been suckling on them, drawing cries of tormented delight from her whilst his hand covered the wet heat of her sex and his fingers teased an open eager passage.

The secret betrayal of his thoughts and his body had felt to him as much of a betrayal of his duty to protect her as it was of the duty that lay on him towards his future bride and their marriage.

He had been angry. With himself more than with Sophia but it had been on her he had vented his anger, telling her savagely, 'It can't be me. You already know that, Sophia. I'm engaged to be married.'

'An arranged marriage,' she had reminded him. 'Not a love match.'

Something in the truth of her words had turned a knife in his heart as sharp and destructive as one of the fine jewelled daggers favoured by his ancestors, cruelly sharp knives that could rip out the heart of a man and still leave that heart beating and the man breathing. For a while.

'My marriage is my concern, and as for it not being a love match, it will be my duty and my pleasure to learn to love my wife and to teach her to love me. My very great pleasure.'

His words had been cruel. He had seen that in the look in her eyes. He had taken a step towards her, Ash remembered, and then he had stopped as she dashed away the tears she hadn't been able to control. A child's tears, and if he had been cruel then it had been to protect that child.

And now as then, Ash wanted to turn and walk away from her, but somehow he couldn't, just as he couldn't drag his gaze from her or stop his body reacting to her. His own weakness lashed at him, biting deep into his pride. But still he looked, still he let his senses fill with the pleasure of her.

Her dark curls caressed the bare shoulders revealed by her figure-hugging goddess-style amber-gold silk dress with its diamante waistband, her velvet-soft eyes sparkling, her lips warm and invitingly parted. They would taste of sensuality and promise, and her low-cut gown would be no barrier to the man who was determined to enjoy exploring the soft warmth of her naked

breasts. But that man would never be him. Sophia was
the sister of one of his closest friends; she was passionate and emotional. To bed her would bring complications into his life that he didn't want. And why would
he need to bed her when he had so many other willing
women to choose from who understood that sex was
all he required from them? Sex and nothing more.

Oblivious to the turmoil of Ash's most private
thoughts, Sophia looked over at the table where her
parents were seated with some of their guests. As always it was her father who was commanding everyone's
attention whilst her mother looked on, her blonde head
inclined towards him, her whole manner one of calm,
controlled formality. Just as her father demanded. Just
as the husband he had chosen for her would demand of
her. She was not her mother. Her own nature was far
more turbulent and intense. Still focusing on the table,
she told Ash with fierce desperation, 'My father thinks
he can argue me into giving way. But I won't.'

Ash could hear the desperation in her voice. Against
his will he found himself thinking that she reminded
him of a beautiful butterfly beating her wings against
the iron bars of a cage that imprisoned her, her desperate attempt to find freedom destined only to leave her
crushed and broken. Unexpectedly, for all the gossip
about her hedonistic lifestyle, there was still an innocence and vulnerability about her. Against his better
judgement he realised that he felt sorry for her, but he
knew her father and he knew that King Eduardo would
not give up his plans easily. He was as traditional and
old-fashioned a father as he was a king, ruling his family and his country with the firm belief that they were
his to command and control and that their duty was to

obey him in all things. He did feel sorry for her, he allowed himself to acknowledge. Yes, but it was not his business and there was nothing he could do, other than offer her a reminder of the reality of what being royal meant.

'As your father's daughter you must always have known that ultimately he would arrange a marriage for you to someone he considers to be suitable?'

Just for a minute Sophia was tempted to drop her guard and admit to him that the kind of marriage of which she had always dreamed and for which she had always yearned was one based on mutual love, not dynastic necessity. But she knew that if she did that she might easily betray to him what she did not want him to know. She had her pride after all, and she certainly wasn't going to have him feeling sorry for her because she wanted…

What? Love from the one man she knew would never give it to her? No. She might have wanted that once as a foolish sixteen-year-old but she did not want Ash now.

But she did want to marry a man she was in love with, a man who loved her back, and she was prepared to wait until she found it.

Only when she stood before her chosen bridegroom, ready to give herself to him in the sacred intimacy of marriage, would she finally be free of the scorching pain of Ash's rejection.

But as yet she had not found that man or that love, and it certainly wasn't for a lack of trying.

Watching her, he saw a bleakness in her eyes, and Ash felt himself filled with an unexpected compassion for her. She had been such a sweet child, so loving and giving, so sweet in her hero-worship of him. She had looked up to him as though he was a god. Childish adoration from a girl who had desperately wanted her father's love and been denied it, that was all. He was not a god and she was no longer a child. He owed her nothing. Right?

She was not a child any more, he reminded himself. She had stopped being a child to him that fateful afternoon when she had begged him to take her virginity.

Who was the man who had taken it and her? Could she even remember his name? Given what the gossip columns had to say about her, Ash doubted it.

Sophia swallowed, knowing that she had to make one last attempt to secure his help. 'Ash, all I want from you, all I want you to do, is behave towards me tonight as though you want me—not just to share your bed, but potentially as the wife everyone knows you must ultimately take in order to give Nailpur an heir. You are such a matrimonial prize that my father is bound to drop the Spanish prince if he thinks that there is any chance he can marry me to you. You have everything my father admires—royal blood, status and wealth.'

For once Ash was lost for words. When Sophia had said that she needed his help it had never occurred to him that she meant she wanted help of that nature for the kind of plan she had just outlined to him. She had a shrewd brain, he acknowledged. She was completely right in her assessment of her father.

'Ash. I *need* you to rescue me and be my prince in shining armour just like you used to rescue me when I was little,' Sophia continued in a voice made husky with impassioned need. 'Do you remember that time I nearly drowned when I followed you, Alex and Hassan along that rocky cliff face?'

Against his will Ash could feel the tug her words were having on his heartstrings. 'That was a long time ago,' was all he permitted himself to say.

'I still remember it,' Sophia told him softly. 'I was nine years old, and when I slipped into that deep pool you jumped in and rescued me. Alex laughed at me but you carried me back to safety. You made me feel safe and protected.' Yes, he had then, she thought, but later... later he had hurt her so badly that even now... No. She mustn't think about that tonight. She must only think of her plan, the plan she had been working on from the minute she had learned that Ash was coming to the engagement party and she had seen a possible way out of the trap that was closing round her.

Ash frowned. There it was again, that echo of vulnerability in her voice, that admission that was like a private memory, a private awareness shared only between the two of them, as though he was the only one she could allow to see beneath her shell.

Sophia let some of her pent-up breath ease out of her lungs, the release unwittingly causing her breasts to swell softly over the top of her gown.

They were fuller than they had been when she was sixteen, and even more tempting in their allure, Ash recognised, irritated with himself that he should be so aware of them. His memory supplied him with an intimate mental image of the dark crowning of her nipples, erect and hard, pushing against the fabric of the dress she had been wearing, showing him how much she desired him. That had been then, Ash reminded himself, and now he was old enough and cynical enough to know one woman's body was much like another, and that physical desire once slaked soon evaporated, leaving him bored with the woman he had previously wanted.

Imploringly, Sophia reached out and placed her hand on Ash's arm. Immediately his body reacted.

In an attempt to distract himself he tried to focus on her hand and not his own feelings. He looked down at where Sophia's small hand lay against the sleeve of his expensively tailored, dark coloured Italian linen suit. Her nails were buffed to a natural sheen, and against his will his mind recorded for him the way he would feel if she were to rake those nails against his back in the intensity of her ecstasy. Sweat dampened his chest beneath his shirt from the heat pounding through his body.

'Our father is allowing Alex to choose his own bride, so why should I have to submit to having my husband chosen for me?' Her brother's engagement had come as a complete surprise to her, and to Carlotta, the sibling to whom she was the closest. 'You loved Nasreen. Why shouldn't I be loved and love in return within my own marriage?'

The passion with which she spoke confirmed what he had already told himself about the emotional intensity she would bring to her sexual relationships. Such emotions had no place in his life any more, and he was determined that they never would. And if he could have her without those emotions? If they could enjoy each other now as the sexually experienced adults they both were? The rush of fierce male urgency that surged though his body gave him its own answer. But then there had never been any doubt about his awareness of her as a woman from the minute he had turned round tonight and seen her coming towards him.

In fact, if he was honest, Ash couldn't remember ever before having such an immediate and insistent ache of hunger for a woman to the extent that it came between him and the cool logic of the business affairs to which he gave priority these days.

He had to distance himself from her.

'My marriage is my business,' he told her curtly, as he fought against his reaction to the thought of taking her to bed.

She had done it again, Sophia recognised. She had trespassed into a private place where she was not welcome. Because he still loved Nasreen?

That pain she could feel in the region of her heart was simply caused by the fact that if her father succeeded in marrying her off to this prince, she would never know what it felt like to be loved in that way. It wasn't for any other reason—such as her wishing that it was Ash who loved her. Certainly not. She wasn't sixteen any more. And neither was she going to let the subject drop. To her family she was the rebellious 'difficult' one, the one who was always challenging the status quo and pushing their father, the one who bit harder than anyone else. That was her reputation and she wasn't going to abandon it now just because Ash was looking at her in that forbidding, icily cold way.

Nasreen. Ash wished that Sophia hadn't mentioned her name, but she had.

He had vowed that he would love the bride who had been chosen for him, and that their marriage would be one of mutual, total faithfulness to each other. Loving the woman who had been promised to him in marriage from childhood had been a matter of great pride and honour to him, and a duty that he had taken seriously.

Orphaned as a young boy, he'd been brought up by an elderly nurse, whose stories about the great love affair between his great-grandfather and his English bride had built a responsibility within him to love and cherish the young maharani who would one day be his bride. Love mattered more than anything else, his nurse had told him. He must love his bride and she would love him back, with that love making up for the loneliness he had known as an orphan. After listening to his nurse he had believed when he married he would love his bride as completely and faithfully as his famous warrior ancestor had loved his.

Had that belief sprung from arrogance or naivety? He didn't know. His mouth twisted in a grim expression of bitter self-contempt.

He only knew that the harsh reality of his marriage and the death of his wife—a death for which he believed that, in part at least, he had to carry a burden of blame—meant that he would never, ever again allow emotion into any intimate relationship he had with a woman. Never again would he mix sex and love. Never. Sex was a pleasure and a need, but it was just sex. He could allow himself to want a woman but he could not allow himself to love her.

CHAPTER THREE

Ash must still love Nasreen very much indeed to react to the mere mention of her as he had just done, Sophia decided.

How she hungered to be loved like that, wholly and completely, as herself and not for her royal blood. One day, one day she would find that love, Sophia assured herself fiercely, just so long as she remained free to look for it, and wasn't forced into a marriage she didn't want. Her passionate nature, like molten lava compressed for too long beneath unforgiving stone, pushed against the unspoken rules of never betraying any real feelings in the Santina family. Before she could stop herself she had burst out, in self-betrayal, 'My parents don't believe that love matters. Duty to our family name is all that counts. Especially to my father.'

The pain in her voice caught Ash's attention. He knew her history so well that he could easily recognise the real reason for the way her voice had trembled over those telling words...*my father.*

What was happening to him? He had a thousand more important things on which he ought to be focusing. The negotiations he had been involved in to turn the empty, decaying palaces which had once belonged to minor, now long-dead members of his extended family into elegant hotel and spa facilities were at a vitally important stage, as was the exhibition of royal artifacts being mounted by his charity to raise money to help educate the poor of India. These should be at the forefront of his mind, not this wayward passionate and far too desirable young woman standing in front of him.

He needed to bring their conversation to an end.

'I'm sure that your father only wants what's best for you,' he told her as he had done before. He knew that his words were bland and meaningless but why should he try to comfort and reassure her? Why should he care what happened to her? He didn't, Ash assured himself.

Best for her? Wasn't that what he had said to her all those years ago before he had walked away from her? That refusing the plea she had made to him was 'best for her' when what he had meant was that it was best for him.

'The best for me?'

Ash could see the bitterness and the despair in her eyes as she shook her head in rejection of his words.

'No!' The second vigorous shake of her head that accompanied her denial had the dark cloud of her soft curls and waves sliding sensuously over her bare shoulders, reminding him… Reminding him of what? Of how much his body was still aching for her?

'What my father wants is what he thinks is the best for him and for the Santina family. And as far as he's concerned I've always been an unwanted and unexpected addition to the family.' The softness of her mouth twisted painfully as she challenged him. 'You know that's true, Ash. You know the gossip about…about my birth as well as I do.'

It was true. He had been a boy, invited back for the
school holidays with Alex after Alex's mother had realised that he was an orphan with no family with which
to spend the long holidays from their British boarding
school; Sophia herself had barely started school when
he had first heard the rumours that the king might not
be her father.

'You have the Santina looks,' was all he felt able to
say to her now.

'That is what my mother said when I asked her if it
was true that the English architect everyone gossiped
about might be my father, but doesn't it tell you something that never once whilst I was growing up did anyone ever suggest I should have a DNA test?'

'What it tells me is that both your parents were so
sure that you are their child that a DNA test wasn't necessary.'

'That's what Carlotta says,' Sophia admitted, 'but
then with an illegitimate child of her own and her
refusal to say who the father is, she would say that,
wouldn't she?' Normally Sophia wouldn't have been
so outspoken about Carlotta's situation. The birth of
Carlotta's son, Luca, had meant that she, too, was out
of favour with the king. They both felt they were outsiders and this had bonded them together, despite the
fact that Carlotta had a twin sister.

'And Carlotta has always been very sensible.'

Sophia gave him a wry look. 'You call having a child
out of wedlock by a man who she won't name and, ac-
cording to our father, bringing disgrace on the family
sensible?'

A child—a son—only he knew how atavistically he

longed for fatherhood, Ash acknowledged as he felt the familiar strike of sharply savage pain burning into him.

He had assumed when he and Nasreen had married that she would be as keen to start their family as he had been. Initially, when she had told him that she wanted to delay it because she wanted to have time alone with him he had been charmed and captivated. But then he had learned from Nasreen's own lips the real reason why she did not want to have a child—ever—and that had led to the first of many rows between them.

To outsiders, his desire for children would be seen as the natural desire of a man in his situation to have an heir to follow him. There was an element of that there, of course—he had a duty to his inheritance, after all— but his need went deeper and was far more intensely personal than that. The loneliness he had felt as a child had made him long for a family of his own in a way that had nothing to do with being royal, and it was a need he could not turn away from or deny. One day he would marry again—it would be a marriage of practicality and not emotion, but the children that came from that marriage he would love, because that love would come naturally and not have to be forced, or pretended. As he had done with Nasreen. The bitterness of his failure to love Nasreen still brought him guilt.

'It isn't what one would have expected of Carlotta,' he acknowledged.

'No, Carlotta was always the good one. Not like me. I suppose if anyone outside the family had to choose one of us to do something disgraceful to our father they would choose me.' Sophia pulled a face. 'Oh, don't bother denying it. We both know that it's true. If it had happened to me I'd do exactly what Carlotta has done and insist on keeping my baby. No matter who tried to take it away from me.' Her face softened as she added, 'Little Luca is so gorgeous that sometimes I almost wish he was mine.' There was genuine warmth and tenderness in her voice. 'Not that my father would ever tolerate such a lapse from what's expected from me. It would be the last straw, I expect, and he'd probably completely disown me.'

'I doubt that your father would be trying to arrange a suitable marriage for you if he himself wasn't convinced that you are his child, especially not to a fellow royal.'

His statement was intended to reassure her, as well as bring their conversation to a halt, but instead of doing that, it had Sophia firing up again and telling him fiercely, 'If you think that then you don't know my father at all. It isn't for my benefit that he wants this marriage. It's for his own. For the Santina name. That's all that matters to him. Not us. Just the reputation of the Royal House of Santina. It's always been the same, all the time we were growing up. All he ever said to us was that we must remember who and what we are. He rules us as he rules the kingdom, because he believes it is his right to do so. Our feelings, our needs, don't matter. In fact, as far as he is concerned we ought not to have feelings at all, and that applies especially to me. He doesn't understand me, he never has. You could help me, Ash. It wouldn't take very much. As I've already told you my father would drop the Spanish prince like a hot potato if he thought he had any chance at all of marrying me off to you.'

'I doubt very much that your father would switch his

allegiance, son-in-law-wise, on the strength of seeing us together for a handful of hours at a party.'

'Yes, he would,' Sophia told him succinctly. 'And I'll prove it to you if you help me.'

Sophia's problems were nothing to him, Ash reminded himself. He was simply here as a friend of her eldest brother. The fact that he had felt a certain amount of protective compassion for Sophia as a young girl didn't mean anything now. After all, then he had been an idealistic young man looking forward to a future filled with love and happiness, or so he'd thought. Now he was a realist—an embittered hard-hearted realist, some might say—who knew that such dreams were exactly that. Wasn't the truth that it was his view now that an arranged marriage worked better, lasted longer and fitted the purpose it was designed for—the production of an heir and the continuation of a family name—than so-called love? Wouldn't his own second marriage be exactly that? After all, one only had to look at Sophia's parents to see the strength of such a union. Whether or not the rumours about Queen Zoe and the young architect were true, their marriage remained solid, as did their shared dedication to preserving the Santina family name. If Sophia thought that her father would ever sacrifice that to allow her to make a marriage of her own choice then in his opinion she was wrong. Besides, she was grown-up now, and could take care of herself. And he didn't want to muddy the waters of diplomatic relations with a poorly timed flirtation.

'I don't see the point in us discussing this any further, Sophia.' He pushed back the sleeve of his dinner jacket to look at his watch.

He had extraordinarily sexy hands and wrists, Sophia

acknowledged, and the warm tone of his skin only emphasised that. For months after he had rejected her she had soothed herself to sleep at night imagining those hands on her body in a caress that was warm and loving, as well as sensually erotic. The pain of the sudden sense of loss that swept her locked her breath in her throat.

'I have to leave soon,' Ash told her. 'If you spoke to your father about your feelings I am sure that he will give you more time to get to know the man he has chosen for you.'

The fierce shrug of her slender, tanned shoulders in a gesture of denial and despair caused the strapless top of her dress to slip downwards, so that the shadow of the areole of her nipples was clearly visible to him. Desire hot and feral shot through him. What was the matter with him? It was as though his body was taking delight in deliberately disobeying the orders he had given it, as though his own flesh was actively delighting in punishing him by making him…want her?

Anger gushed through him. With a figure like hers she must surely have known the risks of wearing a dress like that.

'If you don't want everyone here to see what I can see right now I suggest you do something about your dress,' he warned her curtly. 'Unless, of course, you do want every man in the room to see what only a lover should be permitted to enjoy.'

Not understanding what Ash was saying, Sophia stared at him in confusion and then took a step towards him, gasping as she stepped on the hem of the front of her dress and felt it slide down her body.

Instantly Ash moved towards her, shielding her from

everyone else's sight, his hands on her upper arms so that no one could see what she now knew must be clearly visible.

She had sunbathed topless as and when appropriate in front of any number of people, so why right now did she feel so embarrassed and self-conscious, her hands trembling as she tried to tug up the front of her dress, succeeding only in dislodging it even more. She choked, 'You'll have to help me—I need you to reach round and unfasten the hook and eye at the back so that I can adjust the front.'

He wanted to refuse but how could he without letting her guess the effect she was having on him, as though he was a callow youth who had never seen a woman's naked breasts before.

It was just as well the elegant ballroom was so busy, Ash acknowledged as he reached around behind Sophia almost as though he was about to take her into his arms, deftly unfastening the hook and eye and then lowering the zip.

'That's too much,' Sophia protested, her face burning as she felt the top of her dress fall away. Not, thankfully, that anyone could see that. Not with her virtually pressed up against Ash in the way that she was, his arms around her.

'Pull the top up, then I can fasten the zip,' he ordered her.

'I can't, you're holding me too close,' Sophia complained.

Exhaling impatiently, Ash started to step back only to have her grab hold of his arm and tell him frantically, 'No. Don't move, everyone will see.'

'I thought that almost everyone already had,' Ash felt

bound to tell her grimly, and then frowned as he saw the speed with which she tried to conceal her expression from him and the hint of tears that had dampened her eyes. She was genuinely embarrassed, he recognised as she tried desperately to stay close to him and at the same time tug up the top of her dress.

'Here, let me help.'

He had only meant to put the top of her dress back in place but somehow his hand was cupping the side of her breast, his fingertips accidentally grazing her nipple.

Fiery flames of male hunger burned at his self-control. Because his bed had been empty for too long, that was all, whilst an involuntary shudder of sensual awareness openly seized Sophia's body.

Silently they looked at each other, and then looked away, neither of them willing to speak.

Why on earth had that happened? Sophia asked herself, still shocked by her reaction to him. She didn't still want him. How could she when she had outgrown her foolish youthful feelings for him? It had been an involuntary reaction of her body to the unexpected intimacy of a male touch, she assured herself. And that male touch could have been any male touch? Yes, of course. Of course.

Silently Ash reached behind Sophia, his expression grim as he refastened her dress, and then stepped back.

He was on the point of walking away from her, his work done and his self-control shot to hell, when he saw that King Eduardo was beckoning them over. Impossible for him to ignore that royal command. Ash sighed and told Sophia, 'I think your father wants us to join him.'

As they had reached the king and queen, champagne was being handed round in anticipation of a toast. Sophia's intense focus on how to get around her father's insistence on this ridiculous arranged marriage had momentarily made her forget that this was her oldest brother's engagement party. His fiancée Allegra's father, Bobby Jackson, got to his feet, albeit rather unsteadily, and made a rambling speech of congratulation to the newly engaged couple. When it finally came to an end, they all dutifully toasted the happy couple, but an uneasy rumble of chatter spread around the ballroom in reaction to Bobby's graceless public display.

'Ash, how lovely to see you,' Queen Zoe welcomed him, the diamonds in the tiara she was wearing sparkling in the light from one of the room's many chandeliers. Sophia's mother was clearly covering her embarrassment with polite small talk.

Deprived of Ash's presence at her side as her mother engaged him in conversation, Sophia had to fight hard not to feel alone and abandoned, emotions that were all too familiar to her growing up, despite the fact that then, as now, she had been surrounded by her siblings. The trouble was that she had never felt truly accepted or loved by them. Because she had never felt accepted or loved by her father? That was why it was so important to her to marry someone whom she loved and who loved her, someone who would share her determination to raise the children they would have in a loving home in which those children would know how much they were loved. That was her secret and deepest desire.

As her father began his toast to the happy couple, Sophia turned to look longingly towards Ash. Only a metre or so separated them but it might as well have been a mile. Listening to her father's speech he had his back to Sophia, and she rubbed her arms in a small sad gesture of self-comfort.

Her father was still talking, and looking straight at her, Sophia realised, as he announced, 'And Alessandro's engagement is only the first Santina engagement we are to celebrate. I am delighted to be able to tell you all that my youngest daughter Sophia's fiancé is shortly to arrive in the kingdom.'

The shock of what her father had said descended on Sophia like an icy wall, numbing her, reducing her to dumb, frozen shock, unable to speak or move as she was jostled by the throng of press photographers who had all been focusing on her brother and Allegra but who were now all around her, instead, their cameras flashing.

As swiftly as it had engulfed her, the numbness receded, leaving her with the reality of the full horror of her situation. Inside she felt as though she was shaking from head to foot, as she was gripped by a rising tide of nausea and furious helpless despair. This couldn't be happening. Her father couldn't have trapped her into an engagement without giving her any warning. But he had, and now she had no way of arguing him out of his plans. She felt so weak and helpless, so lost and alone. Instinctively she looked towards Ash but there were too many photographers in the way. Her father, on the other hand, she could see, and the cold warning look in his eyes told her what he expected of her.

Reporters and photographers surrounded her, pushing mikes and lenses in her face as they demanded a response to her father's announcement.

'I...'

'My daughter is delighted to be engaged,' the king answered for her. 'Aren't you, Sophia?'

Shock and a lifetime of always giving in to her father's will couldn't be ignored or overcome no matter how much she wanted to do so. As though someone else was speaking the words Sophia bowed her head submissively and responded, 'Yes.'

From the queen's side Ash watched and listened to what was happening with a mixture of feelings, the least wanted of which was the sudden savage stab of antagonism he had felt towards the unknown prince to whom Sophia was now officially engaged.

'Such a relief that Sophia has finally seen sense and realised that her father knows what's best,' Queen Zoe murmured to Ash. 'All this gossip about her in the press has made the king very angry. Marriage will do her good. The king believes that the prince shares his traditional values and beliefs on the role of a royal consort and royal children, and will soon have Sophia realising where her duty lies.'

'Sophia…' Sophia felt a small tug on her arm, and she turned from the throng of reporters to see the concerned face of her sister Carlotta.

'I can't believe what Father has done. He knows I don't want to be engaged. I can't stay here, Carlotta,' she told her sister. 'Not now. I'm going to my room.'

By the time she reached the relative sanctuary of her room Sophia's thoughts were in such turmoil that she was trembling from head to foot as though the force of them couldn't be contained within her body. How foolish and naive she had been to think that her father would allow her the freedom of trying to change his mind. That had obviously never been an option. Her father must have known all along that he intended to announce her engagement without her real consent. Now her plan to parade Ash in front of her father, in the hope that the king could be deceived into thinking that there could be a match between her and Ash, seemed so juvenile and ridiculous—the pointless hope of someone who didn't recognise or understand reality. Angry, helpless, frustrated tears blurred her vision. All the things she had done to avoid marriage until she found the right man had been a complete waste of time. She might as well have remained here in her room at the palace as a good and dutiful daughter who never did anything to challenge the status quo.

How was she going to endure what would now be her future? She couldn't, she wouldn't, Sophia decided on the wave of panic and pain that welled up inside her, and she certainly wasn't going to stay here and let her father marry her off. She'd run away and leave the island, cut herself off from her family, before she'd allow herself to be forced into this marriage. Her heart was hammering even faster at the enormity of what she was thinking.

Without allowing herself to think through what she was doing she ran to her wardrobe and started pulling clothes out of it and putting them into a case—something that normally one of the maids would do for her—tears running down her face whilst she did so.

Panting and out of breath she froze when her phone beeped with a text. It was from Carlotta asking if she was OK. About to reply to it, Sophia checked. She didn't want to involve her sister in what she was going to do.

Now all she had to do was get changed and go to the airport. Then within a few hours she would be on her way to London where she had school friends who she hoped would offer her a temporary sanctuary from her father and from her unwanted marriage.

They would help her, wouldn't they? She did have friends. Did she? Who? Those good-time, fun-loving crowds whose lives consisted of moving from party to party?

She'd make new friends. Get herself a job. Anything, just as long as she didn't have to marry the man her father had chosen for her.

She pulled a dress out of her wardrobe and quickly put it on, grabbing a jacket to go over it, mentally checking through what she would need.

Her passport, she had that; some money, she had that. Of course, the national airline would let her board any plane she chose, and with luck it would be morning before anyone realised she had gone, by which time it would be too late for her father to stop her from leaving. By morning she would be on her way to start her new life. A life where she would be in control, and no one else.

'The last flight's gone?'

'Yes, Your Highness. Several hours ago. We had to cancel most of our flights because of the number of private jets the airport has had to accommodate. The first flight to London will be tomorrow morning. I think several journalists are booked on to it.'

Sophia gave a small shudder at the thought of travelling with a curious press pack.

She was well and truly trapped on the island, just as she was going to be trapped in her unwanted marriage.

'Maybe one of the party guests could offer you a

seat?' the young girl manning the enquiries desk suggested with a smile.

'No. I don't think…' Sophia began, only to stop as she remembered Ash telling her that he was going to have to leave the party before it ended because he needed to get back to India. Her heart thumping, she asked the girl as casually as she could, 'Do you happen to know if the Maharaja of Nailpur's plane has left yet?'

The girl consulted a list out of Sophia's view and then told her, 'It's scheduled for take-off in twenty minutes, Your Highness. His plane is waiting at the royal departure gate right now, but the maharaja is flying back to Mumbai and not London.'

Nodding her head Sophia turned away and reached for her suitcase. Ash would help her now, surely? He knew how she felt. He had seen how unfair her father was being. There *was* no one else she could turn to. She wasn't going to ask much of him, just a lift in his plane to Mumbai, that was all. From there she could get a flight to London. Despite the glamorous lifestyle she lived, Sophia was very good with her allowance and did have some savings. Enough certainly to pay for a flight to London from Mumbai, and once there… Once there she would worry then about what she would do. Right now she needed to get on Ash's plane and make sure that he allowed her to leave the island with him.

If the security guards on duty at the doors to the private royal departure and arrivals gate were surprised to see her on her own and wheeling her own suitcase they didn't show it, bowing briefly to her as she walked past them. Their presence and the bow they had given her brought home to her the reality of what she was about to do and how her family and especially her father would view her behaviour. There could be no going back once she had broken the unwritten rules of the Santina family by defying the king. For a moment she hesitated. And then an image of her standing in church beside the stranger her father wanted her to marry filled her head, galvanising her. Her heart had begun to thump wildly just in case someone at the palace had discovered her absence and had realised that she might try to leave the island. The thought of the ignominy of being dragged back to the palace to face her father and his wrath was all Sophia needed to carry her out of the airport building and into the April night air.

In front of her, down the length of the red carpet that had been put out to welcome their guests, she could see the steps to the executive jet with Ash's royal crest emblazoned on its side.

There was no one around to stop her as she climbed the steps to the plane, dragging her case with her. Sophia wasn't used to carrying her own luggage, just as she wasn't used to packing her own things. The case was heavy and she was slightly out of breath by the time she had managed to drag it behind her and into the empty body of the executive jet.

The main cabin of the plane was elegant but business-like compared with some of the private jets on which she had travelled before. It was clear to her that Ash used his plane as an extension of his office when he travelled, but then, unlike some of the men who formed part of the smart set with whom Sophia partied, Ash was primarily a businessman, despite his title. At the far end of the cabin there was another door. Sophia went to it and opened it. Beyond it lay a bedroom fitted with a large double bed; a door next to the bed opened into a bathroom. The grey-and-white decor of the main cabin was repeated throughout.

The bedroom area of the plane was in darkness and through the window Sophia could see Ash striding down the red carpet towards the plane accompanied by a uniformed steward. Her heart skipped a beat, tension filling her. She wanted to rush to meet him and beg him for help but he was frowning and looked impatient. Sophia looked towards the bathroom. What if she simply hid herself in there and waited until they had taken off before she revealed her presence to him? That way he would have no choice other than to help her.

The bathroom was compact with a good-size shower and the usual facilities. Most of the spare floor space was taken up by her case so she had to perch on it after she had pulled the door to and taken the precaution of locking it. Presumably there was another lavatory off the main cabin of the jet for staff, so she should be safe in here until they had taken off.

As soon as the jet's door was locked behind him, enclosing him in its cabin, Ash removed his jacket and sat down at his desk, reaching for his laptop. He had work to do ahead of the meeting he was returning to Mumbai to attend. He had planned to speak with Sophia before he had left the ballroom. His deep-rooted sense of responsibility demanded that he at least tell her that her marriage need not be as bad as she obviously felt it would be, but he hadn't been able to find her. And if he had found her? If she had pleaded with him yet again for his help? He pushed the laptop away and stood. He had no idea where it had come from, this persistent unwanted ache of what he refused to call anything but mere male lust, but he did know that neither it nor Sophia herself could have any place in his life.

In her hiding place Sophia felt the plane start to move down the runway and then gather speed, before lifting into the sky. She had done it. She had left the island and it was too late to change her mind now. In the morning her family would know she had gone, and her father... Her father would be furious with her, but if he wouldn't listen to her and let her tell him how she felt then she had no other way of showing him just how much she did not want this marriage.

The plane levelled off. Sophia opened the bathroom door. The bedroom was still in darkness. She looked towards the door to the main cabin and the light showing underneath it. She went towards it and then stopped. She felt so vulnerable and alone. If she went to Ash now she was afraid that she might... That she might what? Throw herself at him and beg him to hold her, to comfort her, to keep her safe? That was ridiculous and it just showed how unlike her real self she was behaving to even think such a thing. It would be better though, wouldn't it, for her to wait a little longer before she did see Ash in order to give herself time to feel less vulnerable.

Ash didn't much care for the new temporary steward who had been taken on while his usual man, Jamail, had gone home to look after his sick mother. The man hovered too much and too closely. There was something in his eyes that Ash didn't like, although he told himself that he was probably being unfair to him as he shook his head, refusing the drink the steward had offered. He looked at his watch. Just gone 1:00 a.m. It was a six-hour flight to Mumbai at least and, with the time difference, it meant it would be 9:30 a.m. before they landed. He had arranged for his meeting to take place in his office in his penthouse apartment in the city, to save time and also to allow him to leave for Nailpur—the Rajasthan state of which he was the ruler and from which he derived his title—the following day to attend to his business there.

A new message from Hassan caught his eye. In it his old friend was complaining that they hadn't had a chance to catch up at the engagement party.

It was true that Alex, Hassan and Ash didn't get much opportunity to catch up with one another in person. They all had busy lives. Ruefully, he emailed back—Perhaps you should get engaged yourself, and throw another party—and then went back to concentrating on the key points he wanted to discuss with the consortium that was going to renovate one of Nailpur's smaller palaces and turn it into an exclusive luxury hotel.

Whilst he personally did not need the money this venture would bring in, the people of Nailpur did. Ash sat back again in his chair as he contemplated the problems he and the highly trained young managers he had hired were having persuading the people of the benefits of growing their crops in a more modern and cost-effective way. For the hotel and the other plans he had to bring tourists and money into the area, which needed to become more self-sufficient. They had the land and the climate with which to grow much of the food visitors would require, but the local farmers were afraid of committing to the new methods of agriculture Ash wanted to introduce. In order to get round that he was encouraging their sons—and daughters—to go to agricultural colleges so that hopefully they would come back and persuade their families to adapt to modern ideas.

The door that led to the small kitchen beyond which lay the flight deck opened and the steward came out asking Ash if he would like anything to eat or drink.

In the bedroom, sitting on the edge of the bed in the dim glow from the brilliantly star-lit sky outside—she hadn't dared switch on the light in case it alerted Ash to the fact that she was here before she was ready to face him—Sophia took a deep breath. She couldn't hide herself away in here forever. She got up, heading for the door into the main cabin, then stopped as she heard voices and realised that Ash was talking to someone.

She couldn't go in there now. She'd have to wait until he was alone. She went back to the bed and sat down on it, stifling a yawn as she did so. It had been a long and exhausting day and the bed looked very tempting. Too tempting to resist, Sophia admitted as she had to stifle another yawn.

Two minutes later, having automatically removed her shoes and her dress, she was tucked up beneath the beautifully welcoming and expensive sheets, her eyes already closing.

CHAPTER FOUR

FOUR o'clock. Another couple of hours or so and they'd be touching down in Mumbai. He might as well get some sleep, Ash acknowledged as he closed down his laptop and then made his way to the jet's bedroom, not bothering to turn on the light as he headed for the bathroom where he stripped off his clothes and then stepped into the shower. Emerging from it he dried himself and then pulled on one of the two thick towelling robes that hung on the inside of the bathroom door.

This time he did switch on the bedroom light and then froze in disbelief as he saw what—or rather who—it revealed.

'Sophia! What the...'

The angry sound of Ash's voice brought Sophia out of her shallow sleep to struggle into a sitting position as she clutched the bedclothes around her naked upper body, and wished that her heart was not hammering so fast.

'I'm sorry, Ash,' she apologised immediately. 'I was going to come and tell you that I was here but you were talking to someone and then I was so tired that I must have fallen asleep.'

This was the last thing he needed right now, Ash

thought. In the intimacy of the cabin he could smell the scent of her skin, lush and warm, subtly demanding that his male senses respond to it as nature had designed them to do.

'You've done this deliberately, haven't you?' he accused her. 'Even though I told you that I couldn't help you. I don't like having my hand forced, Sophia.'

Sophia bristled. How dare he accuse her of that kind of subterfuge and deceit. 'You're wrong,' she snapped. 'I'm not trying to force your hand. I came to the airport thinking I'd be able to get a scheduled flight to London but all the normal flights were cancelled because of the number of guests arriving for the party on their own private jets. When the girl at the airport said that yours would be the first to leave I just—'

'You just got on board? Have you any idea of the diplomatic reverberations your behaviour is going to cause? And not just with your father. How do you think your husband-to-be is going to react to the news that you've disappeared with another man within hours of your engagement to him being announced?'

'He will never be my husband. Never. I wish this was any plane but yours, Ash, I really do, but I had no choice. I will not let my father sacrifice me for his dynastic ambitions. All I want is to get to London. I've got my passport. After your plane puts down in Mumbai you need never have anything to do with me again. In fact, I don't want you to. I thought you were someone special, Ash, a true hero, and someone I could turn to, but you aren't. Stupid of me when I already knew the danger of putting my faith in you and then being rejected as a result.'

He knew immediately what she was alluding to and her criticism stung.

'You offered me your virginity and I refused it for your own sake as much as anything else. You were sixteen. To have taken your innocence from you would have been dishonourable.'

They shouldn't be having this conversation. It took him too close to a dangerous place he didn't want to be.

'All I want from you is a lift to Mumbai,' Sophia told him. 'No one need know that I left the island with you.'

'You're damned right they don't because the truth is that you did not leave *with* me. And why London?'

'I've got friends there.'

She was avoiding looking at him, causing Ash to demand curtly, 'Friends, or a man? A lover who—'

'No!' Sophia denied truthfully. Please don't let Ash ask her if she was really sure those so-called friends would welcome her and help her, she prayed, because the honest answer was that she didn't know.

Now that the shock of being woken up by Ash's angry voice was abating, another and far more dangerous awareness was spreading quickly through her body and that was the realisation that under that robe he had tied so carelessly Ash was probably completely naked. Why should that either concern or disturb her? She didn't want him any more.

And yet she couldn't remove her gaze from where the robe gaped as he paced the cabin floor with angry strides. She could see the shadow where the dark line of hair that bisected his body started to broaden out after it had crossed the taut plain of his belly. Once and only once she had attempted to trace that line, but then she had only got as far as the waistband of the jeans he had been wearing. Now… She was suddenly finding it very difficult to swallow, Sophia realised, and even more difficult to drag her gaze away from Ash's body.

'By rights I ought to instruct my captain to turn this plane round and—'

'No!' So great was her panic that Sophia didn't stop to think as she launched herself towards Ash, reaching out to grasp his arm, her eyes brilliant with fear and pleading as she looked up into his, totally oblivious to the fact that her anxious movement towards him had dragged down the bedding that had been protecting her nudity.

Her breasts were everything he had known they would be, Ash thought, her waist every bit as narrow and her hips every bit as lusciously curved. The tiny bikini pants she was wearing were somehow more a provocation highlighting her sex than a means of covering it. Deep down inside him a truth that refused to be ignored was surging through him. Whether he liked it or not, he wanted her.

In the soft light of the room her skin glowed, her tan contrasting with the white bedding, the lush sensual promise of her body emphasised by the almost monastic and starkness of the decor. Until now he hadn't realised just how much the clinical decor reflected the emotional emptiness of his life. Now, though, the sight of Sophia's near-naked body with its ripe readiness for sex had the effect on him of tightening an already-too-coiled spring of needs and desires that had tormented him all evening.

The plane dropped several feet, catching Sophia off guard as she struggled to pull up the sheet to cover her nakedness, her breath escaping from her lungs in a soft gasp as the movement of the plane threw her towards the edge of the bed.

Instinctively Ash reached out to stop her from falling. Instinctively, and disastrously, because it was her naked body he was now holding and his own was reacting to that fact. He had to let her go. He had to leave this cabin, but instead he was moving closer to her.

This couldn't be happening. It must not be happening, Sophia told herself. But it was too late. It was happening, and somehow it seemed that her treacherous body wanted it to happen even though that should have been impossible.

He shouldn't be doing this. He didn't want to be doing this, Ash told himself, but he was, the lean darkness of his hand cupping one of her breasts whilst his lips feathered tiny tormenting kisses around the nipple of the other.

She wanted to deny him, to stop him, to tell him that this must not happen, but like a sealed jar of sweetly potent honey-infused wine exposed to the sun's heat, the seal on her emotions and needs melted beneath his touch, leaving the sweet wine of her own desire to spill hotly through her veins.

Where did it come from, this instinct that was pure and intense? After all, she had no past experience of this kind of intimacy, no matter what others might think. But now, it had her reaching out to clasp Ash's head between her hands to hold him to her breast whilst her body arched, her head thrown back in an agonised delirium of a desire she wanted to reject but couldn't. A wild febrile urgency possessed her.

Her nipples, sensitised by his touch, and the shockingly fierce tug of his mouth, were sending almost violent spasms of erotic raw need to every part of her body, but most of all to the trembling aching heart of her sex. The pulse that sprung up there was growing more insistent, more urgent, more demanding, with every touch of Ash's hands and mouth. It was as though, deep within her, the womanhood she had told herself she had guarded so assiduously for the man who would love her and take away the pain Ash's rejection had caused her was pushing against the bonds of her virginity, swelling and softening, pulsing with its female need for the man arousing it so intensely.

Ash groaned. She was everything he had never allowed himself to imagine that she would be and more. Now, with the iron denial he had been trying all evening to forge around his desire for her to seal himself off from it, broken apart by the strength of that desire, he had no need to imagine what it would be like to give in to the lure of her, because he was already doing it.

She smelled of vanilla and almonds, her flesh dew-damp from her own arousal, the dark crowns of her nipples hard eager tellers of female need. He parted her thighs with his hand, caressing their sensitive inner flesh, his own body responding to her shudder of reaction and soft moan of impatient need. He was hard and ready, the head of his erection swollen and taut. Her briefs had bows at the sides which he unfastened with a tug. Her sex was bare to his gaze and touch, her Brazilian wax revealing its delicate shape. He was just reaching out to part its neatly folded outer lips when there was a knock on the cabin door and it started to open.

There was barely time for him to thrust the sheet over Sophia's nakedness and conceal his own body with the robe he was still wearing before the steward was in the room, his eyes widening as he apologised and started to back out, telling him that the captain wanted him to know that strong head winds meant that their flight would be delayed by fifteen minutes or so.

An icy cold revulsion every bit as all-consuming as his desire had been earlier gripped him. How could he have behaved as he had?

'You'd better get dressed,' he told Sophia without looking at her as he started to move away from her. They dressed in silence before moving out into the cabin.

What on earth had possessed her? Sophia felt sick with shock and disbelief, unable to say a word.

Eventually the captain announced that they were coming in to land. Ash hadn't spoken to her once since they had left the bedroom, and Sophia hadn't wanted him to. She was still in shock and bitterly angry with herself for her own behaviour.

His curt warning, 'Seat belt,' broke the silence between them, and had her fumbling with the straps, the colour crawling up under her skin as she caught the look that the hovering steward was giving her. He might not have seen her naked body thanks to Ash's prompt action but he knew exactly what had been happening; his look told her that.

In the past when men had given her that lustful knowing look she had been protected from it by the truth that only she knew—namely that no man had ever touched her intimately or shared her bed—but now thanks to her own betrayal of herself she had no defence against it. And there was no one to protect her from the pride-savaging pain of that. No one. For the rest of her life now she would know and remember how she had let herself down by succumbing to a...a need she had believed she had conquered years ago, Sophia acknowledged as the plane came in to land.

It would be a long flight to London, and she hoped that she wouldn't have to wait too long at the airport before beginning it.

She looked at her watch. At home people would be waking up, and her maid would be discovering that her room was empty and that her bed hadn't been slept in. Her stomach churned, but now more than ever she knew that she could not marry the Spanish prince her father had chosen for her.

Ash was unfastening his seat belt and standing. Automatically Sophia did the same.

'My case...' she began when Ash headed towards the door that the steward was just beginning to open for them.

'Leave it,' Ash told her curtly as he indicated that she was to precede him to the now-open door. 'The steward will attend to it.'

'But I want to get on the first flight I can...' Sophia began, only to come to an abrupt halt, her face paling as she looked out of the door of the plane and saw the camera crews and photographers jostling for position at the bottom of the steps. Paparazzi.

Obviously irritated by the fact that she wasn't moving Ash came up behind her and then stopped himself, cursing under his breath as he saw the press waiting for them below.

'I suppose this was your idea. Run away in secret and then let the world know what you've done,' he told her angrily.

'No. It's got nothing to do with me,' Sophia defended herself, but she could see from the look Ash was giving her that he didn't believe her.

There no escape for them, Ash recognised. To retreat back into the plane now would only increase the gathered press's hunger for their photographs. They had no option other than to try to outface them.

'Come on.' He took a firm hold of her arm.

No matter how much she might long to persuade herself that Ash's hold on her arm was protective it just wasn't possible, Sophia acknowledged miserably. Not after she had seen the anger in his eyes.

As they neared the bottom of the steps the waiting reporters started firing a barrage of far-too-intimate questions at them, demanding, 'Is it true that the two of you are an item and that you've left a fiancé behind on Santina?'

'Have you any comment to make on the fact that you've spent the night together?'

'Does King Eduardo know that the two of you are together?'

'Are you together, or is the princess going to go back to her fiancé?'

'Did you enjoy your in-flight entertainment, Your Highness?'

The last comment given with a knowing leer as a camera was lifted to catch her expression was too much for Sophia's control. She turned towards Ash, instinctively seeking his protection as she clung to his arm and turned her face into his chest.

'Thanks, darling,' the photographer called out. 'Great shot.'

'So I was right. You did engineer this,' Ash accused Sophia in a savage undertone. 'Have you no sense of dignity or shame? What do you think it's going to do to your own reputation, never mind your father's and your fiancé's, when this...this circus of predators splash their photographs all over the world? Or don't you care?'

'I didn't do anything.' Sophia tried to defend herself, her voice catching on a small hiccup of misery. She was trembling as much with the hurt of Ash not believing her as with the anxiety caused by the unexpected and unwanted presence of the press. She was, of course, used to being besieged by the press; she was even used to them asking her very intimate questions about her personal life and the men she dated, but then she had had the protection of knowing that no matter what they chose to believe and publish none of it was true. Now, though, things were different. Now she had been seen with Ash in a very intimate situation, indeed. 'Why would I? I don't want my father to know that I'm here. I don't want him to know anything until I'm safely in London.'

'Well, no one else could have organised it.' Ash only began to frown as out of the corner of his eye he saw the steward sidling up to one of the reporters who handed him a fat envelope, whilst the steward glanced furtively over his shoulder.

It looked very much as though Sophia was telling the truth, Ash had to admit, but there was no time to question the steward now or, in fact, to do anything that would draw further press attention to them, he decided.

'This way,' he instructed Sophia, still holding her arm as he pushed his way through the crowd, almost dragging her with him as he headed for the waiting limousine.

'What's this for?' Sophia demanded when she saw it. 'I need to be in the airport sorting out my flight to London.'

'And I need to be in my office for a very important meeting,' Ash countered, 'which is where we're going right now, unless of course you want me to leave you to be eaten alive by the press. We can sort out your on-ward flight later.'

The thought of being abandoned by Ash to deal with the ever-hungry-for-gossip paparazzi had Sophia get-ting into the waiting limousine without another word of protest.

The car was soon speeding through the city streets. Sophia had never visited Mumbai or India before, al-though she'd always wanted to—and not just because the subcontinent was Ash's home. She was genuinely interested in what she could see beyond the car win-dows and couldn't help turning to Ash and murmuring, 'Everything's so colourful and vibrant. It makes every-where else I've been seem pale and uninteresting.'

They'd come to a halt in the traffic and out of no-where a boy appeared with a bucket of water and pro-ceeded to clean the car's front windows, despite the driver's dismissive wave for him to stop.

A tender smile softened Sophia's face. Thin and wiry, the boy gave her a wide smile, his brown eyes sparkling when he realised that Sophia was watching him, and quickly came round to her side of the car.

Watching her as she dug into her handbag, Ash felt something he didn't want to acknowledge catching on his emotions.

Nasreen had thoroughly disliked the poor of India, and had made no attempt to conceal her contempt for them.

'Here you are.' He dug into his own pocket for some change, knowing that she would not have any Indian currency.

The car had started to move again.

'Oh, make him stop, Ash, so that I can give the boy the money,' Sophia begged, giving Ash a smile nearly as warm as the one she had given the boy when he did as she asked.

It would be unbelievably easy for a man to be seduced by the warmth of such a smile, Ash acknowledged. And by Sophia herself, as well? He shrugged as the question arose, knowing full well as he did so just how much his body was still aching from the denial he had imposed on it.

They were out of the centre of the city now and travelling on a road along a sea-facing promenade. On the other side of the road Sophia was surprised to see that the buildings had a distinctly art-deco flavour to them, but before she could ask Ash about this they were climbing along another road into what Sophia could see was a very exclusive-looking residential area filled with expensive modern apartment blocks.

Sophia wasn't totally surprised when the limousine came to a halt outside one building that looked even more expensive than the rest.

'My case,' she reminded Ash, avoiding the hand he held out to her to help her from the car. She simply did not dare to touch him, not with every bit of her still aching with longing for him.

'The driver will have it sent up to the apartment,'

Ash told her. He looked at his watch, mindful of his appointment. It shouldn't take too long for him to organise a suitable flight to London for Sophia. He could, of course, have left her to fend for herself but that wasn't Ash's way. He had been brought up with a strong sense of responsibility towards his heritage and a duty to those who depended on him. That was part of the role into which he had been born as maharaja.

When he had children, a son, an heir—as he must— he would make sure that whilst that child understood the duties that went with the privilege and the wealth he would inherit, he would not be burdened by them. A child needed to be allowed to be a child. And between parent and child there needed to be love, as well as mutual respect. As an orphan he had missed out on that love, but even having parents did not guarantee it. Sophia was the proof of that.

Sophia. There he was allowing himself to feel sympathetic towards her again. His footsteps ringing out on the cool marble of the floor to the foyer of the apartment building, Ash paused to turn round to look at her.

Her dark hair was softly tousled, her face free of makeup, her eyes dark and luminous with curiosity as she studied her surroundings. Her lips parted slightly.

To his chagrin, desire, raw and fierce, and definitely unwanted, kicked through him, causing him to turn away from her as he told her curtly, 'The lift is this way.'

Reluctantly Sophia followed Ash. She'd have preferred it if he'd simply left her at the airport to make her own arrangements to board the first available flight for London. The lift, like the building itself, was very modern in glass and steel, and Sophia wasn't surprised when she followed Ash into his apartment to discover a large open-plan living space with a whole wall of glass and a terrace beyond it, both with panoramic views. Nor did the decor of cool whites, charcoal greys and strong matt black surprise her, either. It was all so very masculine. Like Ash himself? A dangerous twist of sensation ached low down in her body.

'Sit down. I'll organise some breakfast.'

'I'm not hungry,' Sophia refused. 'All I want is to get to London. I wanted you to leave me at the airport and not bring me here—' She broke off as her mobile chirruped the arrival of a message, her body tensing. They'd know at home by now that she wasn't there.

Ash had left her and she was on her own in the room. She reached for her phone, seeing immediately that the text she'd received was from Carlotta.

OMG, Sophia, her sister had written, what were you thinking? You being caught in bed with Ash is all over the internet. And I mean all over. There are reporters here and they're grilling Father about you joining the mile-high club with Ash. He didn't answer them, of course. He just stormed out the room. He's really angry, Soph. And humiliated. I hope it was worth it. In my experience, though, it never is.

Quickly Sophia deleted the message, her fingers trembling and her heart pounding.

In the kitchen of Ash's apartment the television was on showing a bulletin from a local English-speaking news channel. The sight of his own face on the screen had Ash stopping to watch.

A reporter was explaining that following the press discovery of Ash and Sophia together on his jet an announcement had just been put out by a spokesperson for the Santina royal family to say that, regrettably, when Princess Sophia had informed her father that he was about to be asked for her hand in marriage, he had been unaware of her whirlwind love affair with the Maharaja of Nailpur and had assumed that she was referring to another royal suitor.

The matter had now been clarified however, and the king was pleased to announce that Princess Sophia was engaged to be married to the maharaja.

Leaving the kitchen abruptly Ash returned to the living room of the apartment, reaching for the control to reveal the concealed TV screen.

'I've found a flight with a seat on it but it doesn't leave until this evening,' Sophia told him. She'd have preferred an earlier flight and it went against her pride to have to accept Ash's hospitality for longer than she wanted.

'Watch this,' he commanded grimly, ignoring her words as he switched on the TV which was running a weather bulletin.

'What—?' Sophia began, but Ash shook his head.

'Wait,' he said tersely.

For what felt like a small eternity Sophia stood in silence in front of the TV screen, not daring to move because of Ash's grim manner, and then she heard the news reader's announcement.

'There is sad news to report for Mumbai's match-makers because today the King of Santina has announced that his daughter the Princess Sophia is to marry the Maharaja of Nailpur.'

With a growing sense of disbelief and horror Sophia watched and listened as the news item Ash had seen earlier was repeated.

Only when it had finished did she turn to Ash and tell him shakily, 'You'll have to speak to him, Ash, and tell him—'

'I shall certainly have to speak to him, and the sooner, the better, but he obviously felt he had no other choice,' said Ash coldly. 'There's only one person responsible for this situation, Sophia, and that person is you. You put yourself on my plane.'

There was nothing she could say to refute that, no matter how much she might wish to. Ash was opening his smartphone. He looked so grimly angry that for the first time in her life Sophia felt that she was facing a man who was even more formidable than her father. Far more formidable, in fact. This was Ash the maharaja, Ash the leader and the ruler of his people. This was an Ash who instinctively she knew would stop at nothing to defend the probity and honour of his royal role, and a quake of very real apprehension made her tremble inwardly.

The speed with which his call was put through to King Eduardo told Ash that the king had been expecting it. Indeed it was Ash's opinion that the royal spokesperson had given the statement he had specifically to ensure that Ash did contact the king.

'Ash.' The older man's voice was harsh and Ash suspected the use of his own first name intended to make him a supplicant for the king's forgiveness rather than an equal.

'Highness.' Ash still responded formally, though. 'There has obviously been a misunderstanding.'

'A misunderstanding?' Anger grated through the king's voice. 'There's no misunderstanding about the fact that you have publicly shamed this family and Sophia's fiancé.'

'I understand your anger, Your Highness, but I can assure you that nothing happened that either you or Sophia's fiancé need be concerned about.' Ash spoke crisply whilst Sophia listened, white-faced and feeling far more distressed than she wanted to admit to.

Was it because of that, because of what he could see in her agonised expression, that he told her father in a more conciliatory tone, 'The truth is that Sophia was overwhelmed by the unexpectedness of your announcement of her engagement. In a moment of panic she boarded my plane unbeknownst to me, intending to make her way to London. An impulsive, ill-thought-out action, I acknowledge, but without any intention of causing anyone embarrassment.'

'And you discussed this together in bed on board your plane, did you? Do you take me for a complete fool? Sophia may not want to get married but she has no choice. And that's her own fault. She's never out of the gossip columns, with her name linked to a different man every week, and now this.'

Her father was speaking so loudly and angrily that Sophia could hear what he was saying. Her face burned, and she might be hurting inside but she wasn't going to defend herself. Her father didn't understand her, he never had.

'Well, there's only one thing to be done now,' said King Eduardo. 'You must marry her yourself, and as quickly as possible. Unless and until you do, she will no longer be considered a member of this family. If you don't marry her then I shall disown and disinherit her. She's brought more than enough shame and trouble on this family. The only way she can redeem herself now and put a stop to this appalling gossip is by marriage to you.'

There was a sharp click as the king ended their call without giving Ash the opportunity to reply.

CHAPTER FIVE

THE king had put him in a completely untenable position and Ash could see from Sophia's expression that she had heard what her father had said. For himself he could feel the ferocity of the opposing emotional claims at war within him. His pride baulked at the thought of anyone, even a fellow royal, dictating to him what he had to do. Yet his own sense of duty to his heritage, to his friendship with Sophia's brother, and in a sense to Sophia herself, to save her from the disgrace and humiliation she would suffer if he refused to marry her, told him what he must do.

'My father doesn't mean what he just said,' Sophia told Ash unsteadily. Her father's statement had shocked her, but what had shocked her even more was the swift pain it gave her to have to contrast her youthful dreams of what marriage to Ash would be like and the harsh reality of what was happening now. Then she had dreamed romantically of a relationship filled with love and happiness. The bitter taste of the ashes of those foolish dreams clogged her throat. 'We can't marry, Ash.'

'We don't have any choice,' Ash responded brutally.

'I want to marry for love.'

'You lost the right to make that choice when you hid yourself away on my plane.'

His words hurt, but hadn't she told herself all those years ago that she would never allow Ash to hurt her again, and that she would be completely immune to him? Immune to him? Just as she had been in the cabin of his plane. It should be her face that was burning but instead to her chagrin it was her body that was engulfed by heat at the memory her thoughts had brought her.

'I lost it the minute I was born,' she countered tartly, but Ash made no response.

Looking at him and seeing the resolution etched into his hard expression, the apprehension she had felt earlier turned into a much stronger fear. Just as those unwanted shocking moments on the plane had shown her a side of herself and the power of her own sensuality that had overwhelmed her, what was happening now was showing her a side to Ash that as a child and then a teenager she had never considered. As she had recognised earlier, the man in front of her was Ash the royal prince, the leader of his people, a man who would allow nothing to stand in his way of doing what he thought was right for the responsibility he owed to his people. Right now, she suspected, that included her, hence that icy trickle of fear that had just run down her spine.

A fear that was reinforced when Ash told her coldly, 'I am in the middle of some very important business negotiations with people to whom the morals of those with whom they do deals are very important. If I don't marry you my reputation as a man of honour will be damaged. I cannot allow that to happen. I have a duty to my ancestors—and more importantly, to my people. Their future, the education of their children and their childrens' futures depend to a large extent on me bringing more money into our local economy and keeping it there to provide better opportunities for them. All that will be prejudiced if it becomes known, as it most assuredly will, that your father has insisted that I marry you and I have refused. That is the way it is amongst people of our inherited status and blood, Sophia. You know that as well as I do.'

Every word he said confirmed what she had already recognised. Now she knew exactly what his priorities were and they certainly weren't her feelings.

Ash turned away from Sophia and looked out of the window.

This was the last situation he wanted, but he had no choice. The honour of his name had to come before his own personal feelings. And he had to marry someone. In the eyes of the outer world, their outer world, his marriage to Sophia would be seen as a businesslike and wholly acceptable decision. He had to have an heir. He had always known that. An heir created with Sophia in a dutiful coming together for that purpose? For an unguarded second he remembered how it had been between them on board his plane. He tried to close down on that memory but it was too late. Without looking at her he heard himself telling her more openly than his need to control his reactions liked, 'We may both know that a marriage between us is not what either of us would have chosen, but since we have no choice, at least on the evidence of last night, we will share a mutually pleasurable sex life. And as I am sure you will know from your own experience, good sex enhances the lives of those who share that good sex.'

Good sex? Experience? Was this what her dreams of a marriage grounded in true love had been reduced to?

A buzz on the outer door to the apartment halted him momentarily to say, 'This will be my appointment. Once it is over I shall set in motion the arrangements for our marriage. Under the circumstances, the sooner and the more quietly it takes place, the better. From your father's point of view and our own, presenting the world with a fait accompli will bring an end to the current gossip and speculation far more speedily than a press announcement that we are to get married in the future. Once we are wed we will retire to Nailpur. I have business to attend to there, and the privacy it will give us will allow at least some of the gossip to die down. When you return to society you will do so as my wife.'

'And the mother of your child?' Sophia asked him, dry-mouthed.

'Yes. If life chooses to bless us with your speedy conception.' He paused and then gave her a look that stripped her pride bare as he told her, 'Let there be no doubt about one thing, though, Sophia, and that is that from now on you will behave in a way that befits a married woman, who is faithful to her marriage vows and her husband.'

'A marriage that is empty of love, and to a husband I have not chosen for myself?'

'It is as a direct result of your own behaviour that we are now in this situation,' Ash stated coldly. 'And as for love, it is the last thing I will be looking for in our marriage—or outside it. For the sake of the children I hope this marriage will be one they can respect and one which does not dishonour either them or their family name.'

So much pride, so much importance placed on duty, and no place left for love. But he had loved Nasreen. And buried his heart and his capacity to love with her?

Why should she care? She had her pride, too, and it certainly would not allow her to want Ash's love. Before she could comment on the flat cold statement he had just delivered, there was a brief knock on the door and a member of Ash's staff entered.

'Highness, I am sorry to disturb you but Mr Alwar Singh is here with his accountant and solicitor.'

'Thank you, Kamir.' Nodding his head, Ash went towards the open door, saying as he did so, 'Mr Singh, please come in,' and extending his hand to the smartly suited middle-age man who was shown into the room. He was followed by an elegant dark haired woman dressed in a beautiful salwar kameez, and another business-suited man.

'I am sorry to have kept you waiting. Please allow me to introduce you to my fiancée and wife-to-be, Princess Sophia of Santina, before we begin our meeting.' Ash turned towards Sophia, smiling at her as he did so. But Sophia could see that the smile did not quite reach his eyes. Formality and the business of protocol and good manners were no strangers to her, and it was easy for her to step forward to accept the good wishes of Mr Singh and his companions.

She knew why Ash had introduced her as he had, of course. He had just made their marriage to each other official and placed it in the public domain, and now there was no going back from that declaration.

'Kamir, please ask the kitchen staff to serve tea in

my office,' he instructed the waiting staff member before turning to her and saying politely, 'Please excuse us, Sophia.'

'We shall try not to keep you apart for too long,' Mr Singh told her with a smile as the group departed.

She was alone in the clinical vastness of the now-silent room. Alone with her sick dread of the emptiness of the future that lay ahead of her and her despair at the loss of the goal she had promised herself she would one day achieve.

Her glance fell on her mobile and she remembered her sister's message. Numbly she picked up her phone and quickly texted Carlotta. Am to marry Ash. And then she switched her phone off. She had too much on her mind to dare to allow herself the interruption and complication of other people's views and input into the situation, even someone as close to her as Carlotta.

The door opened. She looked up quickly, her heart racing, only it wasn't Ash; it was a staff member who had come to ask her if she would care for tea or coffee.

'Coffee, please.' She thanked him, and went back to her lonely thoughts.

In his office, even though he was doing his best to focus completely and only on what Alwar Singh had to say to him about their proposed business venture, Ash knew that in reality his thoughts and his concentration were divided. He was committed now publicly, as well as privately. Sophia would be his wife. His body responded with a surge of male heat. He wasn't going to make the same mistake again, though. This marriage would be based on practicality and the need for him to have an heir. There would be no love involved. And no question of Sophia continuing with her present hedonistic lifestyle.

Alwar Singh's accountant was running through some of the figures that would be involved in the transformation of the currently derelict palace into a world-class hotel.

'You will, of course, have a forty percent share in the hotel.'

'Fifty percent,' Ash checked her firmly. 'That was our original agreement.'

'It is Mr Singh who will be putting in most of the money and bearing the larger part of the risk.'

'Not so,' Ash contradicted her. 'As Maharaja of Nailpur I have a responsibility towards my people and towards the cultural inheritance left to me by my ancestors. If the unique historical value of the palace is damaged in any way by its conversion to a hotel, something irreplaceable will be destroyed, not just for the present but for the future. That is my share of the risk.'

After the meeting had concluded, his visitors left and Ash turned his concentration to the matter of making the necessary legal and practical arrangements for his marriage.

In the drawing room of the apartment, Sophia threw aside the English language newspaper she had been attempting to read. Freed from the powerful determination of Ash's presence her own independence was beginning to reassert itself. Her independence or her fear? What did she have to fear? She would only need to fear marriage to Ash if she was still vulnerable to him through her emotions, through the love she had once had for him, and that wasn't the case. It was simply her desire to control her own life and to make her own decisions that was filling her with this increasing sense of urgency and need to escape. And why shouldn't she escape? Why shouldn't she prove to herself that she could be strong enough to claim her right to her freedom of choice. She already knew that there was no point in trying to make Ash understand how she felt. Her feelings didn't matter to him.

The staff member who had brought her coffee had returned and was removing the tray. Before she could change her mind, Sophia told him, 'I'd like my case, please.'

The man nodded his head and withdrew.

She was running away again, she knew, but Ash had made it plain that he intended to marry her, leaving her no alternative.

Ash had just finished putting in place the arrangements he had needed to make when one of his staff came into the office.

'The Princess Sophia, she has asked for her suitcase, Highness,' he told Ash.

Sophia swung round when the door opened, her heart banging into her ribs when she saw that it wasn't the man with her suitcase who had come in but Ash himself. One look at his face told her that he knew what she planned to do.

Sophia took a deep breath. Very well, she would just have to make it clear to him that she wasn't going to give up her freedom.

'I don't want to marry you, Ash,' she told him. 'I don't think it's the right thing for either of us.'

Ash could feel the fierce surge of his anger slamming into him.

'You are supposed to be an adult, Sophia, but you are behaving like a child—a child so selfish and self-obsessed that she thinks only of herself.'

His accusation appalled her.

'If you refuse to marry me now after I have introduced you publicly as my fiancée, the damage that will do not just to my role as the leader of my people but to those people themselves will be impossible to repair. Here in India we place great store by certain values—honour, duty, responsibility and the respect we have for our forebears, and what we owe to them in terms of the way we live our own lives.

'You are the one who is responsible for the situation we are in, and you have a duty to that responsibility.'

He was right. What he was saying was true, Sophia recognised. With his coldly angry words he had drawn for her a picture of herself that she didn't like, and that filled her with shame.

She gave a small jerky acknowledgement of her head, and told him shakily, 'Very well.'

She looked so alone and vulnerable, so in need of someone to protect her. Against his will the desire to comfort her invaded him, compelling him to take a step towards her. Abruptly he stopped himself. He had to think of his people and his duty. He had to put them first.

'You give me your word that you agree that this marriage between us must take place?' he pressed her.

'Yes,' Sophia agreed. Her mouth was so dry that the word was a papery rustle of sound.

'Good. Normally it takes thirty days after one regis-

ters one's wish to marry in a civil ceremony before that
marriage can take place, but in our case that require-
ment has been waived and our civil marriage will take
place tomorrow.'

Tomorrow? Sophia's heart jerked against her ribs.

'I have informed your father of our plans. We have
agreed that in lieu of the formal marriage ceremony we
might have been expected to have, a post-wedding reception will be held later on in the year, either in Nailpur
or Santina.'

Ash reached into his pocket for the box he had picked
up on his way back to the room, telling Sophia as he
handed it to her, 'I have this for you. The ring is a family heirloom and may need to be altered.'

Sophia stared at the imposing-looking velvet-covered
box with a crest embossed on it. Taking it from him, and
determined not to let him see how much it hurt her that
he wasn't even attempting to make the romantic gesture
of opening the box and placing the ring on her finger
himself, it was all she could do to pretend to be enthu-
siastic. But as she opened the box she gasped at what
she knew was the largest and most flawless diamond
she had ever seen. Pear shaped and on a thin platinum
band it had to be priceless. A family heirloom, he had
called it. Did that mean…?

'Was this your first wife's engagement ring?' she
asked him, her voice and her body both stiff with the
distaste of being second best.

Guilt and anger dug into Ash's insides like red-hot
wire. 'No. It belonged to my great-grandmother.'

He had never offered Nasreen his great-grandmother's ring, a ring given to her by his great-grandfather as
a symbol of their love. Nasreen had told him that she

longed to wear the enormous emerald ring that was part of another suite of jewellery, and against his better judgement he had allowed her to have it. Against his better judgement because it was a formal piece meant to be worn with the rest of the set.

Somehow it seemed right that Sophia should have the ring that had been a gift of love. His own thoughts made him frown.

Thankful that she wasn't going to be wearing Nasreen's ring, Sophia removed the ring from its box and slipped it on to her own ring finger, surprised to discover that it fitted her perfectly.

It fitted her and suited her, Ash recognised, as he looked down at where his great-grandmother's ring shone on Sophia's finger as though it had found its rightful place.

'Alex texted me to ask what is going on,' he told her, changing the subject. 'Your father obviously told him that we are getting married. I should warn you that I've told him that meeting up again at his engagement party made us both realise that we had feelings for each other that we couldn't ignore.'

'Alex thinks that we're in love?'

'It seemed preferable to telling him the truth. He and I may be old friends, but you are still his sister. I felt it was wiser all round to allow him to think that our marriage is based on a mutual desire to be together, which brings me to another point. Having told him that, I think that in public it will be for the best if we behave as though we want to be together. I have no wish for our marriage to become the subject of any ongoing gossip and speculation, and given that your father publicly announced your engagement to another man, the press are bound to be curious. The discovery that our feelings for each other are stronger than mere friendship will provide the necessary explanation. And that goes for anything you might say to your family.'

'But if my father has told them that he has insisted that you marry me...'

'He hasn't, and he agrees with me that the sudden discovery of our love for each other will provide an acceptable excuse for him to give to the prince. In the eyes of the world this marriage will work, Sophia. Make no mistake. I am determined about that.'

It was over, done. Now, standing here in this anonymous public building that was the marriage registry Ash had chosen, in the eyes of the law she had become his wife. It had been a civil ceremony so plain and direct that against all her expectations she had found in the exchange of the words that had committed them to each other a meaningful simplicity that had touched her emotions. Instead of feeling deprived because she was not having the exotic glamour of a three-day-long traditional Indian wedding, or the pomp and ceremony of being married in the cathedral on Santina, during the ceremony she had thought of all those couples who had made the simple commitment they were making out of love for each other. And that was the cause of the sharp up-rush of pain she felt? Yes, of course it was. What else could it be? It certainly wasn't because she was still foolish enough to dream of being loved by Ash.

They had signed the registry, their signatures had been witnessed, and Ash had told her that her father intended to break the news to their family that their marriage had now taken place later that evening.

'Carlotta will say that I should have waited.'

'And you will tell her that our love for each other meant that we couldn't.'

To step out into the colourful bustle of the busy street as Ash's wife felt almost surreal. There had been no couture wedding gown for her, just a simple white linen dress, its colour drawing a look from Ash that had told her how little a claim she had to its virginal purity.

It was too late now for her to change her mind. They were married. Desperate to distract herself from the anxiety and the feelings of being unloved and totally alone in the world that were beginning to engulf her, Sophia looked around at her surroundings once their car had pulled away from the registry office. It would be impossible not to be excited and entranced by the verve and colour that was India, or to have one's heart captivated by it, she acknowledged. She desperately wanted to share with Ash her wonderment and belief that she would very quickly grow to love her new home, and to ask him questions about the city and of course about his home of Nailpur, but she had to remember that this was a dynastic marriage of convenience. Ash did not want any kind of emotional bonding or sharing between them. All Ash wanted from her was her sexual fidelity and an heir.

'We need to get back to the apartment,' Ash told Sophia. 'We're flying to Nailpur in a couple of hours.'

A new text beeped into Sophia's phone. From her mother this time and not Carlotta. Darling, your father and I are so pleased about you and Ash. I remember how you used to adore him when you were young. Be happy.

Be happy? That was impossible.

Another text had arrived, this one from Carlotta, demanding, Are you sure you're doing the right thing?

Hitting Reply, Sophia wrote defiantly through the emotion threatening to close up her throat. It's a dream come true. Have loved Ash forever and couldn't be happier.

Couldn't be happier, she had told Carlotta, but wasn't the truth that she couldn't have been more unhappy?

Ash stared out of the window. He had done the right thing, the only thing given the circumstances, in subjecting his decision to exactly the same logical tests he would have subjected a vitally important business deal, given the development of a situation that meant that decisive action had to be taken and quickly. Yes, he might have had to make the best of a bad job as it were, but his decision had passed those tests.

So why did he have a niggling feeling that there was something important that he had failed to consider? Why did he feel this wary sense of some kind of danger from which he should retreat? Ash knew the cause of his disquiet perfectly well. It could be traced back to those minutes in bed with Sophia on the plane when he had come so close to relinquishing his self-control. Of almost glorying in succumbing to his own need to abandon that self-control for the sake of the pleasure he had known it would give him to take her without it. That would have been an act as reckless in its way and with potentially as far-reaching effects further down the line as if he had had full sex without using any protection. If he had given in to that need, if he had allowed his desire for Sophia to breach his self-control then... But he had not. The steward's timely interruption had seen to that, and now that he was aware of that possible weakness within him he was in a far better position to deal with it. And he *would* deal with it.

CHAPTER SIX

THEY flew out of Mumbai, its crowded streets swarming with busy life and brilliant with the vibrant colours of its fabrics and decoration that Sophia had already come to feel somehow warmed against the coldness of the loss of her dreams and the harshness of reality that was chilling her heart. It was just after night had fallen, so that below them, the city was a brilliant spangle of multicoloured lights against the darkness of the night sky.

Ash glanced towards Sophia as she sat still strapped in her seat, and looking out of the jet's cabin window. He heard her indrawn breath and saw that they were flying over Marine Drive with its plethora of lights.

'They call it the Queen's Necklace,' he told her.

Sophia nodded her head. After all those teenage dreams of becoming Ash's wife, the mundane reality of the two of them together with nothing of any importance to say to each other was certainly not what her fevered longings had once imagined. But then conversation of any kind hadn't featured in those teenage longings, Sophia was forced to acknowledge, other than a passionate 'I love you' murmured in between the unrestrained passion of Ash's kisses and caresses.

'Nailpur isn't Mumbai,' Ash felt obliged to warn Sophia as they left the city behind and headed west.

'No, I know,' Sophia answered him. 'I loved what I saw of Mumbai but I'm really looking forward to seeing Nailpur and Rajasthan. I read somewhere that the name translates as the Land of Kings. My father would certainly approve of that.'

'Nailpur isn't Jaipur, nor is it any of the other well-known and well-established tourist destinations of Rajasthan. Nailpur is a poor state, its people uneducated, its palaces crumbling. It is my duty to lift my people from that poverty. The days when the maharaja class could live a life of luxury whilst their people endured poverty are not something that can be tolerated any more. And just as it is my duty to lift my people from that poverty so it is also my duty to live amongst them. Your duty as my wife and the mother of my children will be to live with me. So if you were hoping to live in Mumbai—'

'I am not.' Sophia stopped him, too cast down to feel like telling him that as a girl she had read everything she could about Rajasthan in general and Nailpur in particular simply because then she had seen it as a part of him and she had wanted to know everything she could about him.

He couldn't allow this marriage to turn out like his first, Ash thought. No matter what either of them felt, this marriage would endure and not just for the sake of his pride. Only a son brought up to understand and value their family history and the history of their people could truly take his place when the time came.

A royal bride with royal blood was something that his people with their conventional outlook on life, and their belief in the old feudal codes of family and marriage, would expect. He knew that. He had always known it.

A royal bride whose royalty would satisfy the traditional desires of his people.

And a woman whose sensuality would satisfy the desire she aroused in him in a way that his first marriage had denied him?

As always, whenever he thought about the failure and disappointment of his first marriage, guilt gripped him. Must the whole of his life be shadowed by the mistakes he had made then? Nasreen had died because of those mistakes, Ash reminded himself.

The truth was that he had married expecting to give and find love within that marriage and when he had found that love could not be forced by either of them he had retreated from Nasreen. He had allowed her to live her own life because of his own anger and disappointment, because of the blow to his pride of the reality of their marriage, and his discovery that no amount of willpower on his part could ignite the love he had been so arrogantly sure they would share. Because of that Nasreen had died. He could never allow himself to forget that.

Where Sophia was concerned things were different. There could and would be no emotional complications. It was safer that way.

The plane had started to lose height, and below them in the silvery light from the moon and the stars Sophia could see acres of plastic tunnelling of the kind used to grow crops. Turning to Ash, who had been working on his computer throughout the flight, she said curiously, 'I thought this area was too dry for crops and that was why the people were poor and nomadic?'

'It is, but the experts I commissioned discovered an underground river that we've been able to tap into via bore holes and this has allowed us to begin cultivating crops. The people are used to traditional ways and it isn't always easy persuading them to accept new technology. However, I intend to persist. Our water supply is a precious resource, so in addition to educating the people about modern methods of cultivation we also want to educate them to use this resource wisely. The reason I commissioned experts to look into the possibility of an underground source of water was because I'd seen paintings of my great-great-grandfather's indoor bathing pool—it no longer exists but obviously the water had to come from somewhere, and fortunately my guesswork proved to be correct.'

The seat-belt light flashed. Sophia had been relieved to discover that the steward on this flight was not the same one who had been on their previous flight, and she was even more thankful when the plane came to a standstill and the door was opened to see that there were no photographers waiting for them, merely a small group of officials.

Ash had telephoned ahead to his Royal Council to tell them of his marriage, and duly introduced Sophia to them once they had left the plane. As a royal daughter she was well versed in the formality of such things and Ash could see the looks of relief and approval on the faces of his officials as they welcomed her. She had surprised him with her knowledge about the area, he admitted as they were ushered into the waiting limousine, the crest of his ancestors on its door and on the pennant flag flying from the bonnet. Ritual and the preservation of tradition were very important to his senior officials, many of whom could remember not just his parents but also his grandparents before the terrible monsoon floods in the area in which they had been staying had swept them away to their deaths.

Their car left the modern highway which had sped them from the airport through agricultural land and towards the walled city, whose main gate was flanked by huge stone tigers, similar to those in the car's family crest they were now driving. Sophia held her breath. She wasn't quite sure what she was expecting. She'd read of the fabled cities of Rajasthan but there had been very little information about Nailpur, other than a description of its architecture as being typically Rajput in its beauty and richness.

Now, though, as they emerged from the gate in the wall, despite the fact that it was late at night, Sophia could see how busy the city was, the narrow street barely wide enough for the limousine flanked by impressive-looking stone buildings, their narrow windows shuttered and sightless. Up ahead of them the street opened out into a busy square thronged with people. Motorcyclists, often carrying several passengers, eased their way past camels adorned with colourful tassels and enamelled jewellery, their awkward progress accompanied by the stately elegance of the women who accompanied them, the colours and intricate embroidery of their traditional clothing captivating Sophia as she leaned closer to the car window to see them.

Despite the lateness of the hour, the steps to some of the elegant buildings enclosing the square were filled with merchants selling their wares, rich spices, colourful flowers, a joyful display of enamelled bangles. Instead of saris or salwar kameez, the women in the square were wearing brilliantly coloured gathered skirts with tightly fitting blouses, one end of the veils they were wearing tucked into their waistbands then taken over the right shoulder to cover their heads.

Sophia looked as entranced as a child, Ash realised as he glanced at her and saw the way she was leaning towards the window as though anxious not to miss anything. Nasreen had disliked the traditionalism of Nailpur. She had rarely worn Indian dress, preferring Western couture outfits. The sari she had been wearing when she had died had been the cause of a row between them. He had asked her to wear it to a formal event to which they'd been invited earlier in the day in honour of the women of Nailpur who had so lovingly made the beautiful sari for her as a wedding gift. Wearing it had killed her as much as her reckless driving had. He had made her wear it. He had killed her. The old guilt sat within him, a cold leaden weight from which there was no escape even if he had been prepared to allow himself it.

They crossed the square, their progress the subject of curious but discreet attention from Ash's subjects, and then they were going down another narrow cobbled roadway, with women sitting outside doorways attending to cooking pots whilst children played around them. The road widened out, the buildings either side of it becoming larger and far more intricately adorned with filigree balconies and impressive doorways, and then they were in another square and in front of them was the palace flanked on either side by imposing buildings of a similar stature.

As someone who had grown up in a royal palace, Sophia had not expected to be overwhelmed by Nailpur's, but when they had been welcomed into it by a guard of men in traditional dress with huge Rajasthani turbans, she had been unable to stop herself from turning to Ash and commenting, slightly awed, 'How impressive they look and so very fierce. Far more so than my father's uniformed guard. Their turbans are gorgeous.'

'Rajasthan's warriors are known for their ferocity in battle and their loyalty to their leaders. As for their turbans, their style and colour indicates the wearer's status,' Ash informed Sophia. 'That is why these men— members of what was once the Royal Guard—are wearing scarlet turbans that mirrors the background colour of my family crest.'

'They certainly are magnificent,' Sophia responded, pausing as they reached the top of the cream marble steps inlaid with contrasting bands of dark green onyx to ask him, 'I suppose you wore traditional dress for your marriage to Nasreen?'

'Yes,' Ash answered her in a dismissive tone that warned her it wasn't a subject he wanted to discuss. Nevertheless it was hard for her not to imagine the emotional significance of such a wedding with all its history of tradition and culture and the happiness with which Ash must have committed himself to his bride.

What was the reason for the pain that was stabbing through her? Her ability to suffer pain over the realisation that Ash loved someone else and not her had burned itself out a long time ago. Scars sometimes ached long after the original pain had gone, Sophia reminded herself. It meant nothing other than a reminder not to invite that kind of hurt again.

They were inside the grand reception hall to the palace with its alabaster columns decorated with gold leaf, and its marble floor. Long, low, carved-and-gilded wooden sofas ornamented with beautiful, intricate and richly coloured silk cushions stood in elegant alcoves, prisms of light dancing across the floor from the many hanging lanterns suspended from the ceiling. The scent of jasmine wafted in the air and rose petals floated in the ceremonial gold-embossed bowls of water that were brought in for Ash and Sophia to wash their hands.

A maid dressed in a gold-and-cream salwar kameez was summoned to take Sophia to her room after Ash had informed her that they would be eating within the hour.

Upstairs and along a corridor decorated with what Sophia suspected were priceless works of art, she was escorted into what the maid explained to her in halting English were the private rooms of the palace's maharani.

'There is no seraglio here any more as His Highness's great-grandfather married for love and had only one wife. She closed it down, but it is still our tradition that the maharani has her own apartment.'

Behind the fretted and gilded doorway, with its secret 'windows' that allowed those behind it to look out into the corridor beyond without being seen, lay an elegant hallway ornamented with mirrors and alcoves for the lanterns that reflected in them. A pair of highly decorated wooden doors opened out into a much larger room, its polished wooden floors covered in beautiful woven rugs whilst sofas similar to those she had seen downstairs were dotted around the room.

A huge chandelier illuminated the room's vastness,

throwing out sparkling light into the muted shadows of the large room. At one end of it, shutters opened out onto an enclosed illuminated courtyard garden with stairs going down to it from a balcony, the sound of running water reaching her ears from the rill of water below.

'It is very beautiful,' Sophia told the waiting attendant, who gave her a beaming smile in response before telling her in careful English, 'The bedroom is this way, please.'

The bedroom was more European than she had expected, vaguely thirties in its design, with stunning, delicately crafted lamps and light fittings. It had its own wardrobe-lined dressing room and bathroom.

The maid cleared her throat, sounding slightly anxious. 'Please, I take you now to eat with the maharaja.' Sophia stopped exploring her new domain further. She would have liked to have had a shower and changed her clothes before having dinner with Ash but there obviously wasn't going to be time. As she followed the attendant through a maze of corridors she reflected that she needed to contact her family to have the contents of her own wardrobes at home sent over to her.

The girl stopped outside a door secured by two of the turbaned guards who both bowed low to her and then pulled open the double doors.

As she stepped into the room Sophia blinked in the brilliance of the reflected light that filled the room. Every surface within it, or so it seemed, was decorated with a mosaic of glittering metalwork inlaid with pieces of mirror that reflected the light from the suspended lanterns, whilst Ash sat waiting for her on a richly embroidered cushion in front of a low table loaded with a variety of small, tempting-looking dishes.

When Ash saw Sophia gazing around her he explained, 'These mosaic-mirrored rooms were once considered to be a status symbol amongst the Rajput rulers. They are called sheesh mahals, which roughly translates as "halls of mirrors."'

Two waiters stood ready to serve them but Ash dismissed them, telling Sophia after they had gone, 'I prefer to dispense with formality when I can.'

Sophia nodded her head as she took her place on her own cushion. 'I agree, although my father tends to prefer pomp and ceremony.'

'With those who work here dependent on their wages it would be unfair to let them go, but I suspect they find my preference for independence and privacy somewhat bewildering. A need for personal privacy isn't the Indian family way, but it is my way.'

Was he warning her off expecting any intimacy with him other than the intimacy that would be necessary in order for her to conceive?

'The dishes in front of you are a traditional Rajasthani thali,' Ash informed her, 'and mostly vegetarian, although you will find that laal maas and safed maas, which are spicy mutton dishes, are very popular and an important speciality of the Rajput community.'

'It all looks delicious,' Sophia told him truthfully. She loved spicy food and had no hesitation in helping herself to the dishes on offer, although a certain apprehension was inhibiting her appetite. Just for food or for the intimacies of marriage, as well?

It was late when they had finally finished eating; a word from Ash to the staff who had come to clear away

the remains of their meal resulted in the appearance of
the maid who had attended Sophia earlier. As she turned
to follow the waiting girl, Ash leaned towards her and
told her quietly, 'I will come to you in an hour if that is
acceptable to you?'

Her heart started thumping heavily, her mouth going
dry. There was no logical reason for her to be surprised.
She knew why Ash had married her after all.

'Yes. Yes,' she managed to agree, stumbling slightly
over the words, conscious of how gauche she must seem
and even more conscious of how much difference there
must be between her wedding night with Ash and the
wedding night he had shared with Nasreen. Then, no
doubt, Ash would have taken advantage of the intimacy
provided by the soft cushions to pull his bride closer
to him and perhaps feed her morsels of food while he
whispered to her how much he loved her....

She must not think like this. It weakened her and
made her vulnerable and for no good purpose. The past
was the past and she wasn't an idealistic sixteen-year-
old any more. It wasn't being denied Ash's love she
grieved for, Sophia assured herself. It was the love she
had so much longed to find with the man who would
love her as Ash never had and never would. She grieved
for what she would never know because of what she'd
had to do.

Maybe in marrying as she had, putting duty before
her own needs, she was proving to be more of a Santina
than she had previously realised, Sophia admitted as
she followed the maid, whose name she discovered was
Parveen, back to her own apartment.

A silk nightdress was already laid out ready for
her on her bed, and in the bathroom steam rose gently

from the large, sunken, rectangular, mosaic-decorated bathing pool. Rose petals floated on the surface of the scented water.

'Thank you, Parveen. I can manage on my own now.' Sophia dismissed the maid.

An hour Ash had said. It had probably taken them a good ten minutes and more to walk back to her apartment, along the narrow twisting labyrinth of corridors, which Parveen explained had originally been designed to confuse enemy invaders.

In her bedroom Sophia undressed quickly, her hands all fingers and thumbs as her nervousness increased.

As tempting as the warm and fragrant water of her bath was, she didn't dare linger in it just in case Ash arrived whilst she was still there. Clambering from it naked and dripping wet whilst he watched her was hardly going to add to her confidence.

Once she had dried herself she made her way back to the bedroom and looked at the silk nightdress. Ignoring it she wrapped herself in a towelling robe, instead. Maybe the knowledge that she was naked beneath its folds would ignite the same desire in Ash for her that knowing he was naked under his robe had ignited in her for him on the plane.

She could hear footsteps crossing the room beyond the bedroom. Her stomach tensed into tight knots of anxiety. Ash was bound to compare her to his first wife and no doubt find her wanting. Why had she done this? Because she had had no other choice, Sophia reminded herself as the richly painted wooden doors were opened and Ash walked into the bedroom.

He was wearing some kind of beautifully embroidered gold silk robe, its beauty instead of feminising him somehow actually intensifying his masculinity. His head was bare and the shadows of the room threw the sharp angle of his cheekbones into relief whilst concealing the expression in his eyes from her.

He had closed the doors. The room was so quiet Sophia could hear the sound of her own breathing.

'If we are fortunate you will conceive quickly, which will spare us both the necessity of an ongoing intimacy that neither of us really wants.'

He had to make it clear to her that he had not married her out of any desire for her, Ash told himself as he caught the sound of Sophia's indrawn breath. For Sophia's benefit or for his own? Wasn't it true that he had not been able to subdue the ache of need she had already aroused in him despite all his attempts to do so? And wasn't it equally true that right now simply the sight of her and the knowledge of what was to come was accelerating the intensity of that need at a speed that he couldn't control?

But he must control it. He must remember what this marriage was and why he had entered it.

He started to unfasten the closures to his robe—a traditional garment that had been laid out for him by his valet, and beneath which he was naked. Unable to take her gaze off him, Sophia watched with her heart in her mouth as he removed the ornate robe and then came towards her.

He was all male muscle and sinewy strength, long limbed and lean, his body possessed of all the classical male beauty of a Greek statue. She could see the scar on his thigh that she knew must be from a fall he'd had during a polo match that Alex had once mentioned to her. How she had hoarded all those little bits of knowl-

edge about him, how she had clung to them as her own
precious pieces of him, and how her sixteen-year-old
self had hated herself for her weakness in doing so when
he had turned his back on her to go to another woman.
These were dangerous thoughts, taking her back to a
time and place when all she had wanted was to give
herself to Ash. Her heart started to race, the sudden
surging ache deep inside her a growing wash of liquid
heat that caressed her desire every bit as fiercely as she
had once dreamed of Ash caressing her body. A small
sound of female need strained against the taut muscles
of her throat that were denying it a voice.

There was no need for her to question whether or not
Ash was ready to consummate their marriage; she could
see for herself that he was. Her heart was beating so fast
she felt as though it might burst with her need to reach
out and stroke her fingertips along the hard length of
his erection in eager virginal exploration and delight.

A man—another man who was not him and who did
not know that it was merely a practised gesture—would
not be able to help having his male vanity aroused by the
look that Sophia was giving him, Ash acknowledged.
He fought against what it was doing to him, even though
he knew it was a look she must have given innumerable
men before him. Not that he had any right to expect a
past sexual exclusivity from her, and nor did he do so.
They were both adults with their own individual sexual histories. Histories, yes, but he would not tolerate
infidelity from her now that they were married.

It was that thought, the thought of another man
touching her now that she was his wife, that took him
to her side, to untie her robe and push it from her shoulders, his hands sculpting the soft warm flesh of her

body with a feather-light touch. So much lush sensuality was almost too much, Ash thought; it could overwhelm a man until he was trapped in his own desire to possess her. But that would not happen to him, he assured himself, and yet within him there was an urge, a need, to bury his face in the rich dark cloud of her hair, to breathe in the scent of her and then to change that delicate fragrance to something stronger and more elemental as he aroused her. He wanted to stroke his hands all over her, to draw the rigid peaks of her nipples between his fingers until she gasped with the urgency his touch aroused; he wanted to dip into the soft wetness of her sex and taste the juices of her desire for him, and only for him. He wanted… He wanted to possess her as no man had ever possessed her before, Ash recognised, that knowledge thundering through his mind.

He was a man, she was a woman. He had married her so that he could conceive a child with her. It was only because of that that he felt this intense desire to fill her senses and her body. Nothing more than that. It was time he did what he had come to her to do and stop listening to unwanted and illogical thoughts.

For all her lush curves, she was delicately boned and softly light in his arms as he lifted her and carried her to the bed.

His hands tightened on the narrowness of her waist as he laid her on the bed. He reached out and cupped her breast. Her flesh was silky soft and warm, her nipple immediately rising to his palm in stiff supplication.

He rolled her nipple between his forefinger and thumb, seeing her stomach go concave as she sucked in her breath and trembled.

She certainly knew all the pretty little tricks of making her partner feel desired. Well, two could play at that game. He curled the tip of his tongue round her other nipple and then teased it with darting strokes of deliberate arousal. Her whole body trembled, her thighs softening in instinctive invitation. He released her breast to stroke his hand down over her belly and then tease the vulnerable inside of her thigh with the gentle stroke of his knuckles.

Any minute now he was going to possess her. Her body knew that and wanted it, Sophia admitted, but her senses, her emotions, hungered for an intimacy that went beyond mere physical pleasure, no matter how skilled the giver of that pleasure was. She was lost, caught up in the powerful demands of a need that had its roots in the very deepest part of her sexual psyche. A longing she couldn't hope to control forced its way past everything she had told herself this act between them must be in order for her to retain her pride. She wanted, craved, ached for more than Ash's skilled touch against her flesh. She wanted the potency and the passion of his kisses.

Ash started to move between her thighs. As though the words were sprung from some trap deep within her, she heard herself begging him, 'Kiss me, Ash. Kiss *me*.' Reaching for him, sliding her hands into his hair, she pulled his face down towards her own, opening her mouth against his as the fiery hunger of her need spilled through her.

So much passion, too much passion. He should resist, pull back, but the sweetness of Sophia's taste, the quick eager flicking movements of her tongue tip against his lips as though it was a hummingbird unable to survive without the nectar of his kiss, pulled him down, down into a place where his own senses couldn't deny the savagely sensual urge she was creating within him to take her mouth and crush it beneath his own until they were one breath.

Wasn't that dangerous? Because he was afraid that if he kissed her he… He what? He wouldn't be able to stop? No, of course not. Could he prove that to himself? Of course he could.

'If kisses are what you want then kisses are what you will have,' he told her against her mouth as her lips trembled beneath his and the sweet boldness of her daring became an inferno of pulsating need that possessed every inch of her body.

Ash was leaning over her, his hands tangling in her hair as he kissed the side of her throat slowly and gently, and then nibbled on her ear, his thumb stroking the sensitive secret place just behind it.

A soft sound of delight bubbled in Sophia's throat, her eyes wide open and dark with an arousal she made no attempt to hide as she looked at him.

She was the most sensual woman he had ever touched. Everything about her was a hot sweet tide of melting female desire that begged him to complete her. No woman had ever looked at him with such open need, turned to him with such confidence in his ability to satisfy that need. No woman had ever unleashed within him an answering torrent of unstoppable longing for her.

He shouldn't have kissed her. But he had and now he couldn't stop.

He cupped her head to hold her still beneath him and then plundered her mouth in a kiss that stamped her with his possession as surely as though he had penetrated her and filled her body with his sex, until her own sensuality stormed through her, demanding her submission to its needs and to him.

Sophia couldn't contain her own aroused need and delight. Her hands were on Ash's forearms, her fingers curling round them, her body arching up to his in a blatant offer that, driven by his own compelling need, Ash was incapable of refusing.

As the white-hot power of her unleashed passion poured through her, Sophia felt the first surging movement of Ash's body within her own. A fiercely wild sense of joy gripped her. She moved with him, eager for his full possession.

Ash thrust deeper into her and then stopped, in stunned shock and disbelief, as his body fought against what his brain was telling him, the effort it took him to leash his need causing his body to throb with unsatisfied desire. There was a barrier in his way that shouldn't have been there, the barrier of virginity. His brain recognised that. His body, though, ached and pulsed, his flesh demanding that he allowed it to complete what it had started and satisfy its need. But he couldn't. Not now. Not until he knew what was going on.

Lying beneath him Sophia was filled with the urgency of her own unappeased need. He couldn't stop now. Not now when she needed and wanted him so much. Lost in her own desire Sophia had forgotten all about her virginity, but now with Ash pulling back from her and her body still crying out for him she realised what was happening. She had to stop him leaving her. She had to. Female determination filled her as she deliberately tightened her muscles around him.

'You want me to conceive,' she reminded him. 'That's why we're doing this.'

It was true but more than that the movement of her body against his was destroying his attempt at self-control. Ash could feel it slipping, draining away from him as desire for her roared over him. He moved within her, intending to pull back, but somehow his body surged forward and once it had and she was moving with him, making those soft urgent cries of pleasure and need, it was impossible for him to stop what was happening. The barrier parted, the look on Sophia's face as she cried out one of satisfaction and delight rather than one of pain.

Now she had what she had wanted for so long. Now he was hers. Truly hers in the most intimate way possible. Now he had taken what she had always wanted to give him and her body was responding to his possession with the pleasure she had always known it would, wave after wave of it, each one bearing her higher, making her want to take him deeper and deeper within her as she wrapped her legs around him and held him to her more eagerly with each urgent thrust of his possession.

The climax was swift and intense—for both of them—leaving Sophia gasping and shuddering with the intensity of her pleasure as Ash watched her and cursed himself in silence whilst the red mist of his desire for her evaporated to leave him gripped by anger and guilt.

Nothing about his coming together with Sophia had been as he had expected or as he had prepared for. He had expected the sex to be good, but controlled, a coming together of two experienced people who knew the value of sexual pleasure but who would remain free of any emotional involvement in that pleasure. It would be strictly physical, and strictly controlled, but somehow Sophia had got under his skin, and under his self-control. Because Sophia had welcomed him where Nasreen had rejected him, telling him on their wedding night that his love was the last thing she wanted? Telling him that her love had already been given to someone else and that that someone was a married man with whom she had been having a secret affair. An affair which she had no intention of ending and which she fully expected Ash to tolerate and their marriage to cover. It was the way of such things she had told him with a dismissive shrug.

It was the anger he had felt when she had revealed the truth to him that had destroyed not just his physical desire for her but, and far more hard for him to bear, his duty to feel any desire to love her. He had thought that sense of duty so strong and so much an intrinsic part of himself. He had taken pride in it and yet with a handful of words Nasreen had shown him its pitiful weakness. His heart had chilled to her. He hadn't been able to forgive either her or himself for what his reaction to her had shown him about himself.

He had, in effect, turned his back on her, giving in to his own pride and his own feelings about the destruction of his plans for their lives together. And because of that she had died. If he had thought less about the pride he had taken in telling himself that he would love her because it was his duty to do so and instead set his personal standards lower, they could possibly have worked something out—a discreet arrangement of a marriage in which they produced an heir but privately went their own ways. If he had tried harder, been more realistic, maybe they could have salvaged something and then perhaps she would not have died. Instead, he had allowed his emotions to take control.

He deserved the burden of guilt he had to carry. It was his punishment for the pride he had taken in believing that he could create love, not just within Nasreen but within himself, when that power did not belong to him. He had no right to take pleasure in the response that Sophia had given him, and even less to feel that primitive surge of male possessive pleasure to know that he was the one to have brought her to what had obviously been her first experience of the intensity of her own capacity for sensual pleasure.

He could not allow himself to savour that achievement. Instead, he must punish himself for even allowing himself to think of it. And as for his own pleasure? The result of too much abstinence. Nothing more. He could not permit himself to feel anything more.

The darkly bitter emotions that burned inside him turned outwards seeking an escape. He looked to where Sophia lay on the bed, her gaze still awed, her body still sensually satisfied and soft with the aftermath of her climax.

If he went to her now, held her now, kept her close to him and told her of all the many ways in which their coming together had been so very different from anything he had known before, if he told her that she was different from any other woman he had known before… He was already turning towards her, already… Already what? Prepared to break a vow he knew he had to keep if he was to ensure that this marriage worked for the good of his people.

From somewhere he found the will to turn the weak-

ness within him that he didn't want into the anger he
needed. Like Nasreen, Sophia, too, had deceived him,
leaving him to discover a truth that vitally affected their
marriage on their wedding night—even if his discovery
that she had been a virgin was the complete opposite
of Nasreen's revelations to him. And he was grateful
to have that reason to feed his anger because he was
afraid that without it he might be in danger of giving
in to those feelings he had already had to fight back
once. Feelings of tenderness and care, feelings that…
Feelings that meant nothing, were nothing, and which
he would stifle and destroy, because that was the way
it had to be.

Without looking at Sophia he told her coldly, 'I want
an explanation.'

The abrupt coldness of Ash's voice and demeanour
after the sweet hot pleasure of the sensuality they had
just shared shocked Sophia back to reality.

What had happened to her? How and why had she
reacted to him in the way that she had, given everything
she had believed she knew about herself and her desires
for her own emotional future? It didn't make sense that
she should have wanted Ash so immediately, so passionately and so intensely, that it seemed as though her
body had been waiting for this and for him. At least, it
didn't make sense, of course, unless that was exactly
what had happened, and why she had responded to him
the way she had. A cold chill of fear trickled down her
spine. That was not true. It couldn't be true. She refused
to let it be true. So why had it happened?

She didn't know. All she could think, all she could
allow herself to believe, was that there had been a moment—a handful of several long delicately spun-out

golden moments—during which she had felt as though she had touched heaven and held a rainbow of unimaginable delight in her hands. But that had not been reality. That had been a mirage, an imaginary fantasy, that could not and did not exist, and the last dying echoes of the foolish dreams she had once had.

It meant nothing, and for her pride's sake, for the sake of the future, she must now learn to forget about it.

'For my virginity?' she responded in as cool a voice as she could manage. She must not allow herself, never mind Ash, to feel that their coming together had touched her emotions, because it hadn't. As she had just analysed, for herself that reaction had simply been a long-ago echo of something that no longer existed.

'Yes, of course for your virginity.'

She still looked slightly dazed, her eyes huge and dark, her mouth flushed a deep rose pink, but for all the signs of her pleasured sensuality, there was also a vulnerability about her, as though she was in need of… Comfort? Tenderness? These were things he could not give her. White teeth snapping together, he pulled on his robe and went across to the table where the maid had left her a bottle of water in a bucket of ice. He removed and opened it, pouring two glasses, one of which he brought over to her. Water, most precious gift of all to those born into a desert race, because it was the gift of life.

Sophia willed her hand not to tremble as she took the glass Ash held out to her. The water slid coolly down her throat, both reviving her and giving her new strength. Ash watched as a drop of condensation on the glass fell onto her chest and ran down the valley between her breasts. He wanted to look away but somehow he couldn't. He wanted, he discovered, to reach out and stop its descent with his finger and then lick it from her skin with his tongue. He wanted... He wanted nothing other than a marriage of duty and mutual respect through which he could dedicate himself to his people and his responsibility to them.

Sophia pulled the sheet up around her naked body. Ash turned away, an unfamiliar feeling slicing into his gut. She was rejecting him? Why should that bring him such an immediate and intense desire to go to her and hold her, to feel her responding to him again as she had done earlier instead of retreating from him? He didn't know. But he felt as though he didn't know anything any more, and for a man who liked being in control of his life that was intolerable.

He turned back to Sophia. The evidence of the intensity of what had happened between them was plain to see. It was there in the tousle of her dark hair, the flush on her cheeks and the sensual exhaustion in her eyes. She looked like a woman who had been made love to and whose body had shared enthusiastically in that experience. Or did he just see that because it was what he wanted to see?

'It's a bit too late for that now,' he told her brusquely, gesturing to the sheet with which she had so modestly covered herself, 'and I still want an explanation.'

'It isn't a crime to be a virgin, is it?' Sophia shrugged as casually as she could. Despite everything, she recognised that a part of her, that part that still belonged to her sixteen-year-old self, wanted desperately to celebrate the ability of her body to give and receive pleasure, and to know that the wonderment and joy it had given her was shared by the man who had partnered her in it. But of course, to Ash what had happened between them was nothing special. How could it be? She knew that. The euphoria she had felt had gone and all that was left was the chilly reality of what she had lost—not her virginity, but her dreams and her hopes of being truly loved.

'No,' Ash agreed, 'but you have to admit that when a woman goes to as much trouble as you have done to give the world the impression that you are sexually experienced and available, it is bound to raise the question of just why you did so.' Sophia could hear the anger and the bitterness in Ash's voice. 'And I want an answer, Sophia.'

'You already have that answer,' she told him proudly. 'I gave it to you when I told you that I wanted to marry for love. When you rejected me, Ash, I promised myself that I would only give myself to a man who loved me as much as I loved him. That is why I didn't want my father forcing me into an arranged marriage. I wanted to find a man who would love me for myself, and as myself, not as the daughter of the King of Santina.' Sophia paused. Just speaking like this was activating so many feelings she desperately wanted to deny. The temptation not to say any more was great, but something deeper and more demanding was driving her on as though seeking a form of catharsis for her.

'When you reminded me of my responsibility for my actions, for boarding your plane, I realised that I would never reach that goal. But I still have no regrets that I made such a goal my priority. When you rejected me, Ash, when you told me that you didn't want me because you loved your bride-to-be, I was so very envious of her that I promised myself one day I would meet someone who would love me like that and who I could love like that in return. I promised myself then that I would wait for that person. I promised myself that he would be my first and my only lover.'

Why was he allowing her words to cut so deeply into his conscience? The reality was that he had done the honourable thing in doing what she referred to as 'rejecting' her. To have taken her innocence would have been a gross abuse of her and of his own values, even if he had not already been committed to marriage to Nasreen. He had done the right thing, the only thing it had been possible for him to do. He had, in his arrogance, his blind belief that he could order his own emotions and those of Nasreen, given a naive sixteen-year-old the belief that if one waited long enough and believed hard enough that love must appear.

Wasn't he already carrying a heavy enough burden of guilt? Did he have to force himself to carry even more? Was there never to be any peace for him, or any salvation? All he had done was try to emulate the happiness of his great-grandparents' marriage.

A surge of something so intense that it physically hurt him to breathe seared through him—a sense of great loss and regret, sharpened with guilt.

Deliberately not looking into his face in case she gave away more than she wanted to, Sophia continued. 'I knew, though, that if men knew I was a virgin they'd try to get me into bed, as some kind of challenge, so I decided that the best way to hold them at bay was to pretend that I had had loads of lovers. That was why I didn't want my father to force me into a marriage without love.'

Ash had drained his own glass and had gone back to the table to pour himself a second one. Wrenched by guilt, he tried to defend himself to himself with a caustic, 'And do you intend to continue looking for this once-in-a-lifetime love despite the fact that you are now married to me?'

Why was he doing this? Why did the thought of her turning to another man fill him with such a savagery of emotion that it ran like fire through his veins? Because of the disaster that had been his first marriage. Not because of any other reason.

'No,' Sophia denied.

Her voice was filled with so much calm conviction that Ash knew she meant what she was saying. She might claim that she wanted to reject her royal status and upbringing, but right now, no matter how much she herself might deny it should he tax her with it, she was every inch the royal princess bound by her own awareness of the demands placed on her to fulfil her birth role. It was impossible for him not to admit to the respect he felt for her.

Unaware of his thoughts Sophia confirmed her right to that respect when she told him firmly, 'I'm not a child, Ash. When I agreed to marry you I knew what I was committing myself to. It's called growing up. The reality is that I was wrong to think I could persuade my father not to force me into a marriage of which he approved. I recognised that when I heard what he said to you when you telephoned him, just as I also recognised that if I had to have a marriage that would please my father then I would rather it was to you than someone I don't know. Those of us with royal blood aren't always free to follow our own dreams. We have a duty

to fulfil the role for which we ourselves were created
by our own parents.

'If my virginity disappointed you then I'm sorry,
but I am as committed to this marriage and to my own
fidelity to you within it as I would have been had our
marriage been a love match.' That was certainly true.
'I never want any of my children to have to wonder if
my husband is their father. Never.'

Ash closed his eyes. Just for a moment, listening to
her, he had thought…felt…wanted… *What?* Nothing, he
assured himself grimly. Nothing at all. Unable to trust
himself to look at Sophia he picked up his robe and put
it on before turning and walking away from her.

Ash had gone. She was on her own. And she wished
that he was here with her. Wasn't that natural after the
intimacy they had just shared? The *intimacy?* Didn't she
mean the sex? Ash had made the lines that would govern
their marriage clear enough to her and she had accepted
them. Wallowing in self-pity now was as pointless as
looking back at dreams that would only ever be just that.

So what was she going to do with the rest of her life?
What was she going to hang her future on? What goals
was she now going to set for herself?

It wasn't her fault that she'd never been allowed a
proper working role as part of the Santina royal family other than that of appearing at formal functions as
'our youngest daughter.' Given the chance, she'd have
loved to have had an opportunity to get her teeth into
a far more demanding role. She'd once persuaded her
mother to allow her to visit a local school and what
she'd seen there had filled her with enthusiasm for doing
something to help the more needy in their own society,

but her father had thoroughly disapproved of the idea. Now, as Ash's maharani, she naturally had duties that went with that role. Could that be her salvation? Good works instead of love? Love came in many different forms, Sophia reminded herself firmly. Loving Ash's people because they would now be her people and finding ways to help them would benefit her as much as it would hopefully benefit them. Even so, as she contemplated her future, a small shiver of sadness and loss ran across her heart.

In his own room Ash couldn't sleep. The shock not just of discovering that Sophia was a virgin but also of her admission of what her private dreams had been was still sinking in. Now, when it was far too late, he berated himself angrily for not paying more attention to the instinct that had said to him over and over again that there was a vulnerability about her, despite everything he had thought he had known. Why hadn't he thought more deeply about that? Asked more questions, listened to his instincts? Because he hadn't wanted to. Because the demands on him of the past, and Nasreen, overshadowed the present. He had a duty never to forget Nasreen and the guilt he felt about her, didn't he?

It was too late now to wish that he had taken the time to understand Sophia better. They were married, the marriage had been consummated and they both had no choice now other than to make the best of the situation. She had wanted to marry for love, she had said. Well, if she had mentioned that earlier he could have told her that sometimes marrying for love was the worst thing you could do, especially when the other person didn't think of 'love' in the same terms that you did.

He slipped out of his robe and headed for his bed, not sure whether it had been the action of removing it that had brought to mind the way Sophia had looked at him when she had seen his naked body, but knowing that whatever had caused it he wished it hadn't. Being reminded of that right now simply wasn't something he could summon the strength to deal with.

What he'd discovered earlier about Sophia had turned everything he had thought he had known on its head. Lying sleepless in a bed that suddenly felt far too empty, he couldn't hold on to the barriers he wanted to erect against his own emotions. Guilt, pain, a sense of overwhelming loss—he could feel them all.

Moonlight edging in through the unshuttered windows stroked across the faces and bodies of the two people who slept alone and separated. Sophia's hand was on the pillow adjacent to her own as though in her sleep she was reaching for something—or someone. Ash's dreams were vivid with unwanted memories unleashed to torment him. He was a bridegroom approaching his bride on their wedding night. Regret and guilt slowed his progress to where she stood waiting for him, her head bowed, her face veiled. With every step he took towards her the sense of doom filling him grew stronger, but somehow he forced himself to go on. When he reached her he took hold of her veil, pushing it back off her face as she lifted her head.

The sight of Sophia's glowing face looking back him, her eyes warm with desire, her lips soft and parted, filled his heart with an intense relief and joy. He took hold of her, drawing her closer to him, his lips seeking hers as he murmured emotionally, 'Sophia…'

Abruptly Ash woke up, the clarity of his dream still

with him, his heart pounding and thudding into his chest wall. What was happening to him?

Nothing. *Nothing.* And to prove it he would stay away from Sophia's bed until he knew he could take her in it without any shred of emotion threatening his hard-won resolve. This was a marriage of necessity, a marriage that would work because of the duty they both owed to it and to each other. It must not be prejudiced by emotion or by any desire with him that was prompted by any kind of emotion. Once they knew whether or not Sophia had conceived, that would be the time for him to return to her bed. And the ache within him that was burning so fiercely even now must be overcome, because to allow himself to want her was to allow himself to become vulnerable, and he could not permit that.

CHAPTER SEVEN

THEY had been married almost three weeks, and not once since that first night had Ash even touched her, never mind taken her to bed again. Did she want him to? Sophia closed her eyes. It made her feel so humiliated to have to admit how badly her body ached for more of the pleasure he had given it. All those years when she had been able to turn down attempts to seduce her without feeling she was missing out on anything had not prepared her for feeling like this: of lying awake and raw with need in the emptiness of her bed; of feeling her body surge with fierce tight longing just at the sight of Ash's bare throat or arm; of wanting what he had already given her so badly that she had to fight against her need for him. Of course, she had expected to feel like that about the man she loved, but she did not love Ash, he did not love her, and it left a sour and bitter taste in her mouth to know how shamefully she wanted him.

Ash had told her himself that he felt they should wait to see if she had conceived before they had sex again. His uncompromising words had stunned her. He had made it sound as though he didn't want to have sex with her. His words had been a stinging reminder that for him sex with her was merely a duty. That had hurt. In fact, it had hurt so much that even now when her body's evidence said she was not pregnant, she had not said anything about it to Ash. Because she was afraid that now he was married to her, and despite everything he had said to her about duty, he had discovered that the comparison between her and Nasreen was such that he simply could not bear to touch her.

Nasreen. She didn't want to allow the other woman to take up residence in her thoughts and undermine her but somehow she couldn't help it. If Ash could make her feel like that without loving her then how must Nasreen have felt? How much had she delighted in the pleasure they must have shared. As a new husband, Ash would not have stayed away from her bed. The hot surge of jealousy burned her pride. She couldn't allow herself to be jealous of Nasreen. She must focus instead on her own life. So why was she constantly breaking the rules she had made for herself by questioning Parveen about Ash's first wife?

When she had broken the protocol with which she had been brought up and questioned Parveen, the maid had been reluctant to satisfy her curiosity at first, but gradually Sophia had coaxed her into confiding in her. Nasreen had not been well liked by those who staffed the palace, which she rarely visited, preferring to be in Mumbai with her own family, she had been told.

'When a woman marries, her husband's family becomes her family, but the maharani was very close to her family,' Parveen had said.

'But Ash, the maharaja, loved her?' Sophia had asked.

'Yes, the maharaja had loved her very much,' Parveen had replied reluctantly after a small pause, before offering, 'but a man may love more than one wife. For the wife who gives a man his first son there will always be a special place in his heart,' she had added.

And if that wasn't a hint then she didn't know what was, Sophia thought tiredly. Yes, Ash needed an heir. But she had her needs, as well, and right now her pride needed evidence that her husband valued her enough not to humiliate her by rejecting her sexually, because of the intense way she had responded to him.

Today at least she had something with which she could occupy her time and her thoughts.

She was visiting a school in a small village not far from the city, as part of her role as maharani, accompanied by the wife of one of Ash's most important advisers. Aashna, a teacher herself before her marriage, had become Sophia's unofficial lady-in-waiting for such events.

'You may feel shocked by the poverty of the village,' Aashna warned Sophia. 'India is not Europe, and although Ash is doing his best to modernise and educate our children, this will take time. The first generation of young graduates who have benefitted from the schemes he put in place when he came to his maturity are only now returning to Nailpur to help their families. Many of them were agricultural students. Ensuring that we grow enough to feed our people and the tourists that Ash hopes will bring investment to the area will be a vitally important part of our growth towards prosperity.

'We also have doctors graduating to staff our new hospital which will be opened later in the year. Ash has already done much for the people but there is more to do, especially with the young mothers from the tribes.

Their husbands are not always willing to allow them to take advantage of modern health care. The traditional nomadic lifestyle is an important part of our identity and heritage, but it brings its own challenges.'

Listening to her Sophia felt both a huge sense of pride in Ash and all that he was doing and an equally intense desire to be contributing something towards benefitting his people herself.

'The maharani's interest in the new education programme is most gratifying, Highness. My wife is accompanying her today to visit one of the newly opened schools.'

As he signed the final batch of official papers, Ash looked up at his most senior adviser, the words, 'And which school would that be?' spoken before he could stop himself.

'It is the village school at the oasis of the White Dove where some of the children of the nomads are also schooled.'

Nodding his head Ash watched as the older man left the room. It was three weeks since he had married Sophia. Apart from that first all-consuming night, they had spent every subsequent one apart, and most of the days, too. Because he was afraid of what might happen if he went to her? Because he feared the desires, the needs, the emotions she had somehow managed to stir up in him?

It was the shock of discovering that she had been a virgin that had thrown him off guard, that was all. Nothing more than that. He had never intended their marriage to be the kind in which his only contact with his wife was the occasional necessary visit to her bed.

They were partners in the business of being royal, after all, and as his wife, Sophia had a role to play amongst his people. A role which she was already playing without any help from him and playing very well if his most senior aide was to be believed.

Going over to the door Ash opened it and summoned an assistant, telling him, 'Have my car brought round. There won't be any need for an official escort.'

Squatting down on the dusty floor of the single-storey, single-room school, so that she was at the same level as the children, Sophia drew them out of their shyness, communicating with them in their hesitant, newly learned English, watching the excitement and enthusiasm for what they were learning burning in their dark eyes. Their uniform was provided for them by the state, and once she had broken the ice they couldn't wait to tell her how much they loved their new school, their young voices full of praise for the maharaja, whom it was plain they worshipped.

Their innocence and joy caught at Sophia's heart, the sight of their dark eyes and hair causing her womb to contract a little with the knowledge that Ash's children would have that colouring. Ash's children, her children, their children. It would be to them that she would give the outpouring of her love that Ash did not want. They would not grow up as she had done, feeling unwanted and too overwhelmed by the distance that existed between her and her parents to dare unburden herself to them and trust them with her fears.

Engrossed in her own thoughts and the solemnity of the young boy showing her his computer skills, Sophia was oblivious to the silence that had gripped the rest of the room or the fact that behind her the adults were bowing low and moving back in shy awe as they watched their maharaja stride towards his bride. It was only when the boy with her looked up, his eyes widening before he prostrated himself, that she looked round to see Ash looming over her, looking every inch the ruler that he was, even though he was in western dress.

Ash was extending his hand to her, and Sophia was far too aware of the need for royal protocol to be observed in public to refuse to take it. It must be because she had been kneeling down for so long that she felt so dizzy, she decided as she got to her feet.

It was Ash who cordially thanked the teachers for permitting them to intrude on the children's lessons and Ash, too, who shook hands with everyone before exiting the room, leaving her to follow behind him.

Outside, the pungent smell of camel dung stung Sophia's nose. The animals were tethered close to their owners, as the brightly dressed tribeswomen waited patiently for their children to finish their schooling for the day. The nomad women's jewellery jangled musically as they made their low bows to Ash, their odhni modestly pulled across their faces to conceal them, the ends fluttering in the dusty breeze.

'The maharani will travel back with me,' Ash told her waiting escort, turning to Sophia herself to tell her, 'There is something I wish to discuss with you.'

'There is something I want to talk to you about, as well,' Sophia responded.

Once they were together inside the car, though, heading back to the palace, the darkened windows of the limousine somehow made the interior of the vehicle more secluded and intimate. Sophia didn't feel quite as confident about broaching with Ash the possibility of taking for herself a more proactive role in his modernisation plans as she had done when she had listened to Aashna on their outward journey. She couldn't forget how her father had rejected her request to do something on Santina, and how that had made her feel.

Ash looked out of the darkened car window. The sight of Sophia crouching on the floor surrounded by the village children, communicating with them and so plainly loving being with them, had touched a nerve. Only once had he been able to persuade Nasreen to visit one of his schools with him. She had complained that the children were dirty and had refused to have anything to do with them. Ash could still remember the confused, hurt looks he had seen on their faces and those of their mothers. He had sworn that he would never allow that to happen again. Sophia came from a different culture to his own and if anything he would have expected her to be even less inclined to have anything to do with the children than Nasreen. Instead, though… Instead she had reached out to them in such a way that he had seen how happily they had responded to her.

Abruptly he told her, 'My most senior adviser has suggested that it might be appropriate for you to have a formal role to play. I was wondering how you'd feel about getting more involved in the new-schools programme.'

Immediately Sophia turned towards him, her face alight with delight and excitement. 'Oh, Ash, I'd love that. In fact, I was going to ask you if I could become involved. I…I love children.' A small look away from him and a sudden surge of colour into her face told Ash as clearly as though she had spoken the words out loud that she was thinking of their children, of the children he would give her and the children she would conceive for him. The sudden urgency in his body, the slamming thud of his heart and the ache of fierce desire burning in him would have told him exactly what was happening in his own imagination if he hadn't already known.

'I was going to ask you if there was a role that I could play, something that might perhaps relieve you of some of the burden of your own royal duties.'

'There's also the new hospital plan for women and children,' Ash answered her. 'The women, especially those from the nomad tribes, are more likely to be open with you about their medical needs than they are with me. Their culture forbids them contact with men outside their own family circle. In time I want to bring them more into the modern world, but that is complicated and can't be rushed.'

'No,' Sophia agreed. 'Such things have to be handled sensitively. I could perhaps have lessons in their language—just to learn a few words, you know, to break the ice....'

Suddenly the atmosphere in the car had eased, and Sophia felt able to talk easily to him just as she had done when she was younger. 'I want to fulfil my role as your wife, your maharani, as fully as I can,' she told Ash enthusiastically and truthfully. They drove in under the gate which had now become so familiar to her, their car leaving the dust of the open road behind them as the sights and busyness of the walled city closed round them.

'Since you have said nothing to the contrary I take it that...'

Guessing what he was going to say Sophia interrupted him to confirm, 'Yes. That is to say, no, I am not pregnant.'

Tonight. Tonight he would allow himself to go to her, Ash decided. He wouldn't be giving in to an unwanted need within himself if he did. It was, after all, his duty to ensure that he had an heir. Sophia was his. That he should choose to take her to bed to create that heir meant nothing, and did not break his vow to remain emotionally distant from her. Didn't it? Then why was his heart thudding in such a heavy and impatient manner? Why was his body already aching with its need for her? Physical desire, that was all. Physical desire for her and nothing more.

Sophia would have liked Ash to stay with her after their return to the palace but he had business matters to attend to, and as Parveen told her with some excitement, 'many boxes' had arrived from Santina. They were now awaiting her inspection in her bedroom.

Ordering tea and the small sweet biscuits that were a local delicacy and to which she was half afraid she was becoming dangerously addicted, Sophia made her way to her apartment, where the boxes were waiting in her dressing room.

When she opened the first one there was a large rectangular package on top of her clothes with her father's personal seal on it.

Frowning slightly, Sophia removed it and broke the seal, remembering as she did so how as a small child she had been entranced by the 'magic' of stamping her father's seal in hot wax and then applying it to a piece of paper. She had been happy then, before she had realised that there were doubts about her parentage.

Inside the package was a handwritten letter from her father. His letter would no doubt be a reminder of how she should conduct herself and how angry she had made him, Sophia reflected. She was tempted not to read it but she had been brought up with an observance to duty that prevented her from doing that.

Sitting down she opened the letter and began to read it. To her astonishment, rather than being critical of her and angry, her father's words were relatively warm and approving.

'My dear daughter,' he had written, 'I write to tell you how delighted I am by your marriage. It is an excellent marriage and one that pleases me a great deal. To have the ties first established via the friendship Alessandro and Ash shared as schoolboys further cemented by your marriage to him can only strengthen the bond between our two states. Such bonds play an important role in the minds of rulers, which is why I have always stressed to all of my children the importance of the right kind of marriages.

'If I have been overstrict with you then it is because I have been concerned for you. However, I know that in Ash's care you will be well protected.

'I know, too, that our two states can look forward to forging even stronger bonds via their shared business, as well as their shared personal interests.'

The letter was signed with her father's familiar bold and flourishing signature.

The words blurred in front of her as she read them again through the tears she couldn't hold back. *My dear daughter,* her father had called her, even if his letter had turned quickly to the more material advantages he hoped her marriage would bring to Santina.

Such small things really, a kind letter from her father, and an acknowledgement earlier in the day from Ash that he trusted her enough to give her a personal role to play with his people. Neither of them could compare with the great love that had once been her goal, but in their way both of them offered her some comfort and some hope for the future.

A young maid arrived with her tea and biscuits. Smiling at the girl as she quietly left the room, Sophia sat down to drink the tea she had poured for her. When she'd finished, she put down her cup and then stood, ready to sort through the boxes of clothes that had been sent to her from her home.

Two hours later, she and Parveen had opened all but three of them and filled virtually all her wardrobes and cupboard space with the exception of the small row of wardrobes along the dressing room's shortest wall.

'What's left in these last three boxes can go in there, Parveen,' Sophia told the maid, indicating the remaining wardrobes.

Immediately her maid looked apprehensive and uncomfortable as she, too, looked at the narrow run of wardrobes, but made no attempt to go and open them.

'What is it? What's wrong?' she asked her. After a brief struggle where it seemed to Sophia that Parveen wasn't going to answer her, eventually she managed to blurt out quickly, her head down as though she didn't want to look directly at Sophia, 'So sorry, Maharani Sophia, but the clothes of the Maharani Nasreen are in there.'

Nasreen's clothes were still here all these years after

her death. Shock, anger, distaste—Sophia felt them all. A cold shiver ran over her skin, soon followed by an overwhelming feeling she didn't want to name.

Ash obviously loved his first wife so much that he couldn't even bear to dispose of her clothes. They were still stored here in the room that was now *hers*. Nasreen still had Ash's love; she had his devotion, his loyalty. She had probably been inside his head on their wedding night, and it was probably because of his love for her that he had not been able to bring himself to return to that bed. Well, she might have to put up with all of that, but she was not going to put up with Nasreen's clothes in what were now her wardrobes, Sophia decided wrathfully.

'Very well, Parveen,' she told the maid, adding, 'you can go now, I will deal with the rest of my own clothes myself.'

The girl looked relieved to be dismissed, Sophia saw.

As soon as Parveen had gone and she was alone in the dressing room, Sophia went over to the short length of wardrobe doors. Standing in front of them, she took a deep breath and then before she could change her mind she yanked open one of the two pairs of double doors. The draft of air caused by the speed with which she had opened the doors caused the delicate silks inside the wardrobe to move sinuously together almost as though someone was actually wearing them. Sophia closed her eyes. The heavy scent escaping from the wardrobe was making her feel slightly sick and dizzy but as desperately as she wanted to close them and to shut away the sight of the delicate garments so different to her own clothes, once worn by the wife Ash had loved, she couldn't.

Her mood suddenly changed, her earlier fierce, righteous wrath giving way to something more self-destructive and painful. Just seeing the clothes of the woman Ash loved touched those scars within her she knew she must not allow to be reopened. But it was too late. Like serpents escaping from a carelessly sealed basket, the old pain was back.

Reaching out she touched the clothes—red and gold ceremonial saris, sugar-almond-coloured salwar kameez in soft pinks, blues and turquoises. What would she look like dressed in these clothes of another woman? The woman Ash loved. It was as though a terrible compulsion that she couldn't resist had possessed her.

Unable to stop herself she reached into the wardrobe and removed a pale blue salwar kameez set. Like someone in the grip of a dream—or under hypnosis—she walked into the bedroom with it. She was shaking from head to foot. She knew that what she was doing was wrong—for Nasreen, for Ash and for herself—but somehow she just couldn't stop herself, and it made her feel sickened and ashamed of her need to see how Nasreen would have looked. Because Ash had wanted Nasreen, desired her as he did not desire Sophia?

No. She did not care about that, but she had her pride and she and Ash must have a child, a son who would one day continue the royal line. That was how it was for them. And besides… Besides, didn't she herself long for the promise of a new life to love, a child—children—to whom she could give the love she already knew instinctively she would have for them? Quickly she started to undress, despising herself for what she was doing and yet unable to stop herself.

* * *

Walking in the private gardens into which his apartment opened, Ash asked himself why the surroundings which normally gave him so much pleasure and solace, this evening made him feel so alone. Was it because their enjoyment, like the enjoyment of the act of love, should be a shared pleasure? His muscles tightened, his body heavy with desire. Sophia. Just thinking about her was enough to send that desire spilling urgently through him.

Every night since their first as a married couple the memory of the way she had looked at his body had tormented him as he tried to find sleep. He wanted to see that look in her eyes again. He wanted to touch her, hold her, lose himself in her as he blotted out the past while together they created their own shared future in the shape of their child. He wanted. He wanted her.... A tormented groan broke from the rigid tension of his throat. He turned back towards the palace, his stride quickening with impatience, just as his body was quickening with his need.

In her bedroom Sophia stared at the stranger looking back at her from the full-length mirror, a stranger wearing another woman's clothes and smelling of another woman's scent.... The salwar kameez was slightly loose on her own narrow waist and Nasreen must have been a shade taller than her because the fabric was pooling slightly on the floor around her bare feet. The fine silk shimmered as she walked, subtly hinting at the body that lay beneath it, the diamante beading decorating the scarf with which she had covered her head shimmering as she moved.

Experimentally, Sophia draped the scarf over her

lower face, and watched her image in the full-length mirror in front of her. Was this what Ash longed for whenever he had to look at her? Another woman, the woman he truly loved?

He shouldn't be doing this but he couldn't help or stop himself, Ash admitted, too impatient to use the public twisting labyrinth of corridors that led to Sophia's apartments, using instead the passage that his great-grandfather had had installed when the royal apartments had been remodelled so that he and Ash's great-grandmother could come and go to each other without the knowledge of the servants or the need for formality.

The hidden door in the wall of the entrance hall to Sophia's apartment, disguised to look like a painting, opened easily to his touch. He might not normally use the passage but that did not mean that it was not kept clean and in order by his household.

Ash pushed open the door to Sophia's bedroom. And then froze as he stared at the back view of the woman in front of him, not wanting to believe the evidence of his own eyes.

Nasreen. Even though he knew it couldn't be, a surge of the darkest feelings he thought he had ever experienced eviscerated his guts. His first wife had no place here. Just as she had, in reality, no place in his heart? Just as he now had no right to want to forget that his marriage to her had ever taken place? His own thoughts fell into the darkness of his guilt, trapping him ever deeper in its grip.

The woman moved, and instantly he knew.

Sophia.

Only Sophia with that incredible body of hers could move and walk like that.

Anger. A huge rolling wall of it powered through him. Anger against Nasreen for betraying the duty they had owed each other, anger against Sophia for her intrusion into that place within his conscience where even he could not bear to go, and most of all anger against himself. An anger that came out of nowhere, like a desert storm obliterating reality, destroying the landscape within himself, leaving him alone and defenceless against its power and what it had created. In three strides he was at Sophia's side, reaching for her to turn her round, to face him as he demanded, 'Take it off. Take if off *now* unless you want me to tear it from you.'

CHAPTER EIGHT

THE shock of Ash's presence as a witness to something she could only ever want to be private, never mind the fury she could see and feel in him, had Sophia dropping the corner of the scarf, guilt darkening her eyes and burning up under her skin.

What a dreadful thing to happen. It was bad enough that she had been caught by anyone trying on Nasreen's clothes, but that it should be Ash who had found her just at the moment when she herself had tasted the acid agony of shame in what she was doing heaped a humiliation on her that she knew was deserved. No wonder Ash was so very, very angry with her. What she had done was surely a violation of something precious and a privacy that should never have been breached by anyone.

She wanted to apologise to Ash. She wanted to tell him that she had only realised too late what an unforgivable thing she was doing in letting her curiosity and envy of Nasreen get the better of her, but Ash was so angry he wouldn't even let her speak.

The sight of Sophia in Nasreen's clothes made Ash feel as though raw flesh had been ripped from his body, the anger, the shame, the bitterness he felt infusing that guilt with true darkness. He had no right to blame Nasreen and the memory of their marriage for making him feel like this. And no right to feel that he was being cheated of something that deep down inside he ached for, though he knew he had no right to ache for it. Someone or something? He had come here tonight to be with Sophia after far too many long days—and even longer nights—of battling his own inner demons as he fought to allow himself a logical reason for appeasing the need he knew she aroused in him. That might be a need he had no right to allow himself, but tonight, with the future of his name to the forefront of his mind, he had assured himself that being with Sophia, having sex with her, was permissible under the rules he had laid down for himself after Nasreen's death.

Now with the anger boiling inside him, at what unforgivably his senses were now seeing as an unwanted intrusion of Nasreen, and the past into the intimacy he ached to share with Sophia, his guilt could only increase. He had no right even to have such feelings, never mind seek to satisfy them. He had no right to want Sophia. He had no right to anything other than the burden of the guilt he must never, ever forget. And by rights now he should turn round and walk away as a punishment to himself, not returning to Sophia until he had stripped from himself every vestige of personal desire and need for her.

The movement of Sophia's body as she tried to pull away from his hold on her wrist disturbed the air around her, releasing into it the sickeningly familiar odour of Nasreen's scent. He could still remember how it had hung between them on their wedding night after he had realised that he could never love her. Heavy and over-sweet, it clung now to the air, draining it of oxygen, cloying and all-pervading, filling him with revulsion.

'Take it off. All of it,' he demanded again, his voice harsh with the emotional weight of years of guilt, anger and despair added to the even more burdensome weight of his desire for Sophia herself.

Ash released her abruptly, the revulsion he felt for her behaviour written plainly on his face. He couldn't bear to touch her and he couldn't even bear to be in the same room with her. She couldn't blame him for that. What she had done had been unforgivable, but it was too late now to wish that she had been stronger and that she had resisted temptation. If she had... Ash had plainly come to her intending to take her to bed. Against all logic her body reacted to that knowledge with a surge of fierce longing. Longing for a man who'd had sex with her once and then hadn't come near her for three weeks? Sex with a man who had shown her body what sensual pleasure could be, the only man—thanks to the vows she had made—who would ever have sex with her. She was a normal, modern healthily functioning woman, so wasn't it only natural that her body should want to know again that sensual pleasure? Without love? Without respect? Without Ash wanting anything from her other than an heir?

Where was her pride? This was not the right time for them to come together as prospective parents-to-be. She must remember that she was a Santina. She must remember the role to which she was now committed. She wanted Ash to leave so that she could rid herself of Nasreen's clothes and her shame in private. She made to walk past him. She was trembling from head to foot, desperate now to remove the silk garments.

Thinking that Sophia was ignoring him, half maddened by his own unbearable feelings, Ash reached for
Sophia again, dragging her towards him as though the
very sight of her in Nasreen's clothes maddened him
beyond all sanity, tearing the scarf from her, and then,
to Sophia's shock, reaching for the neck of the tunic
and starting to rip it apart.

'No, Ash,' Sophia pleaded with him. He would hate
himself later for the destruction of Nasreen's beautiful
outfit, she knew, and he would hate her even more for
being the cause of that destruction. He wasn't listening to her, though, wasn't paying her any attention at
all, as she struggled in his hold. He refused to let her
go, his knuckles pale against his skin with the pressure
of his grip as he wrenched the delicate silk apart. The
awful tearing sound of the fabric made Sophia cry out
in protest, and as though that one small sound somehow penetrated the red mist of his fury Ash turned his
back to her and ordered her, again, 'Take it off. Now.
All of it.'

From out of nowhere Sophia felt a surge of white-hot
anger of her own rise up inside her to meet Ash's fury.
It burned along her veins swiftly, reaching the unstable
powder keg of her jangling emotions.

'You want me to take it off. Fine, then I will!' she
yelled furiously at Ash as she pulled and tugged at the
clothes that she now loathed so much because of all they
represented, as though they were shackles that bound
and imprisoned her, flinging the garments down on
the floor as she removed them. Her face was flushed,
her temper was up and her dark brown eyes burned
with her emotions. Within seconds the floor around her
was strewn with discarded garments as she hurled them

away from her, and Sophia herself was left standing virtually naked in nothing but her own tiny briefs, out of breath, her chest heaving, the full force of her fury leaving Ash momentarily lost for words. She was. She was… She was magnificent, he found himself admitting, magnificent. Her anger had somehow cleansed her completely of the taint of Nasreen which had so appalled him, just as her feisty removal of her own clothes had left her revealed to him as exactly what and who she was. Herself. Magnificent. And right now he wanted her so badly that the force of that wanting was ripping him apart inside.

'Satisfied now, are you?' Sophia challenged into the silence that had fallen between them, but Ash's unmoving silence had definitely brought its heat down a few degrees.

'Satisfied?' Why was he having difficulty framing the word? Why was his body giving him a thousand messages about just what would bring him satisfaction right now, when it and he knew that he couldn't give in to those illogical needs? And yet… His desire still roiled and thundered inside him, refusing to be subdued.

He took a step towards Sophia and then another, his actions shocking her because she had expected him to leave.

'No, I am not satisfied,' she heard him telling her. 'And I shall not be satisfied until you have conceived our child.'

Then she was in his arms, and he was kissing her, angrily, savagely, humiliatingly, and yet she couldn't find the willpower to resist him. Something within her own anger had ignited a force inside her that was overwhelming all her deep-rooted senses of self-preservation. There was a wildness in the air and in her body, a deep hot fiercely female urgent need that refused to listen to reason and insisted instead that it must and would be appeased. That need was carrying her with it, taking her as passionately as it was telling her that she wanted Ash to take her, as herself, as a woman whose desire was so powerful that it was impossible for him to resist or deny his need to match it. With such thoughts, such hungers, swirling around inside her it was impossible for Sophia to hold on to reality or sanity, especially not when Ash was kissing her with such scorching intensity. Or rather, he was kissing the woman he really wished were here with such scorching intensity, Sophia warned herself.

Under his dark mastery of her senses, and the spell it cast on them, she still couldn't stop herself from responding to him, even though she knew that inside Ash's head the woman on whom he was pouring out his passionate need was cast in Nasreen's image and not her own. All that mattered was the white-hot heat his kiss and his touch were creating inside her. Her body knew him now and knew the power and delight of the pleasure he could give it. Her body had no conscience and no pride, all it knew was that the touch on it was a touch that sent coded messages of past and future pleasure surging along its most intimate pathways, condemning to oblivion anything that might have tried to stand in its way. It was pointless for her to try to tell herself that the fiercely possessive hunger of Ash's touch belonged in reality to another woman. Foolishly her body wasn't willing to listen, not when Ash's obvious desire for it was laying out in front of her a positive banquet of intimate delight. From the curl of his hand in her hair as he pushed it back from her neck so that he could kiss its slender stem, to the strength of that hand on her as he smoothed his thumb over her skin, trapping the betraying rash of goose bumps that gave away her sensual vulnerability to him, every touch aroused a storm of sensual longing and delight.

He should stop, and right now. Every rational and responsible thought in his head told him that; Ash struggled to obey those voices but when he tried to pull away from her Sophia moved closer to him.

Ash was going to leave her but he mustn't. He couldn't. Not when the female hunger and need he had aroused was such an intense longing ache inside her. Sophia wrapped her arms around his neck, pressing small, eager, pleading kisses of her own against the dark sensuality of his throat, shivering with pleasure as she tasted the salty male tang of him on her lips, that taste feeding her appetite for more. His shirt was unfastened at the neck allowing her to slide her hand against the lower buttons and unfasten them, which in turn allowed her to kiss her way along the hard jutting angle of his shoulder.

No. No. A thousand times, no. He might be voicing that denial inside his head but somehow he couldn't bring himself to say those words out loud, Ash realised as his flesh burned raw with the hunger that Sophia's kisses were igniting. How long had it been since a woman had affected him like this, made him hunger and ache like this?

A groan of torment—for past guilts and present longings—tortured his throat. Sophia's kisses, the soft sweetly passionate kisses of a woman to whom the deepest dark mysteries of the raw heat of sexual intimacy were still unknown, filled him with a need to take her and show her how he longed to be touched, how intimately and possessively he wanted to be taken and owned by her feminine desire.

He had never known a need like this, never allowed himself to imagine it could exist. Now he wanted to lie naked beneath Sophia's learning touch, to give himself up completely to her tender exploration, give himself over to her innocent possession. Then when she had had her fill, he wanted to turn things around and show her, teach her, give her the full power of his male desire until their mutual possession of each other took them beyond time and space.

It was too late. Things had gone too far. He couldn't pull back now. He couldn't give her up now. Ash felt Sophia's hand tremble as she battled with his shirt buttons.

The feeling of Ash's chest lifting as he drew in a deep breath and then trapped her hand against his body filled Sophia with despair. He didn't want her touching him. He was going to stop her. But to her shock and disbelief when he lifted her hand from his shirt, instead of releasing it, he placed it flat against the hardness of his erection. For a handful of seconds Sophia allowed herself the erotic joy of knowing him so intimately, of feeling the life force of his maleness beneath her hand, of letting that hand curl against the breadth of his arousal. She felt slightly dizzy, giddy with the swift rush of the responsive desire that was pounding through her own lower body, setting up a rhythm she could feel pulsing into the very heart of her sex.

'Ash...'

His name on her lips was a soft sound of agonised

need, her breath rushing his skin. In the dimly lit bed-room her skin gleamed a soft gold, the almost pagan sight of her naked breasts full and taut, their nipples swollen and dark, wrenching away the remnants of Ash's self-control. In between possessively intimate and erotic kisses he undressed himself, watching with raw male pride when Sophia shuddered softly at the sight of his own naked body, her eyes slipping help-lessly to his sex, her small tremble of longing mingled with uncertainty answering a need in him as old as time itself.

'Touch me,' he commanded her softly. 'Touch me and know me.'

There was something almost hypnotic about Ash's voice, or was it her own desire that was hypnotising her, Sophia wondered helplessly as she went towards Ash. Letting him take her hand and draw her down onto the bed with him where he put her hand back on his body, he told her again, 'Touch me.'

Just the sound of the words was enough to send quiv-ers of eager desire darting through her as she bent to-wards him. The feel of his hard hot flesh beneath her uncertain fingers was both alien and yet somehow in some way already known, as though in her dreams she had touched him like this a thousand plus times be-fore. Each touch, each discovery, each sound of pleasure wrenched from Ash's locked throat felt like a marker put in place on a territory that she had been destined to call her own.

Growing braver, she leaned over and brushed her lips against the taut plain of Ash's flat muscular stomach, hot wilful pleasure possessing her when the slide of his hand into her hair and the raw gasp her touch drew from him told her that despite his stillness his body ached as much as her own.

A few more kisses, scattered daringly against the hair-roughened tautness of his thigh, a tentative caress of the hot tension of his erection, an awareness of the damp heat and the ache between her own thighs, and the coil of need within her had become a full-blown ravening demand.

Inside her head, images formed: the temptation to straddle Ash where he lay and let her body demand the upward thrust of his body into her own and the satisfaction it yearned for, a relentless unceasing hunger that grew with every breath she took.

How long before his self-control broke—how many seconds, how many heartbeats. How much could one man bear and not give in to such an intensity of need? Like a dam breaking, Ash felt his self-control give way. Reaching for Sophia he pulled her down against him, kissing her throat, her jaw, her mouth, taking the sobbed breath of pleasure she exhaled as he covered her breasts with his hands, kneading their soft warmth, letting his thumbs and fingertips mimic the intimate movement of his tongue within the soft damp heat of her mouth,

When he made to lift her on top of him she moved eagerly, almost knowingly, to his guidance, one fierce tremor of her body and the flash of desire in her eyes her response to his removal of her briefs. Her sex was open and naked to his gaze and his touch and it was impossible for Ash to withstand the temptation to caress its soft inviting warmth, his touch drawing a wild shudder of pleasure from Sophia married to a sweetly agonised cry of female longing. The need to pull her down on top of him and pleasure her aroused flesh with his lips and his tongue had Ash sliding his hands along her thighs before he could stop himself, his hunger for the intimate taste of her overwhelming him, as much as Sophia's moan of shocked delight overwhelmed her.

How could she endure such pleasure? How could her body hold back the tide of longing that swept her or the convulsive tremors of preorgasmic sensitivity it unleashed? A fine dew of aching arousal bathed her skin. Her nails raked Ash's skin as he lowered her onto his body, a small mewling sound escaping her lips in her exquisite agony of relief as her muscles welcomed the full hard thrust of him within their embrace, her body rising and falling in concert with his as passion gripped them both.

Without thinking about what he was doing as they lay together in the aftermath of their shared ecstasy, Ash instinctively ran his hand down Sophia's still-damp back, and let it come to rest on the curve of her hip. It was only a small gesture, a natural one, he suspected, for a man who had just shared so much pleasure with his partner, and who wanted to draw that partner closer for the intimacy that came after such intensely satisfying sex, but it was not one with which he was familiar, not one he had ever been tempted to indulge in ever before. Abruptly he withdrew his hand and moved back from her. Moved back but did not leave the bed. They were husband and wife; he was not a machine, and he was certainly not without respect for Sophia or her role in his life. She had just given herself to their marriage, to their commitment to each other to create the next generation, not just with her natural sensuality but also with generosity. He owed her something at least for that.

And that was why he was staying? For Sophia's sake? For the sake of their marriage, for the sake of the duty they had both agreed they would share. For them he would stay, but he would not allow himself the emotional pleasure of drawing her back into his arms to hold her there whilst her heartbeat stilled and he breathed in the warm Sophia-scent of her skin. No, he would not allow himself that, because he did not deserve it.

It was over, and despite the—to her, at least—intense intimacy and closeness of what they had just shared, Ash was already withdrawing from her, still sharing her bed but not touching her, not showing her any tenderness, not saying a word about what to her had been an experience of true unimaginable wonder and delight. And he had wanted what had happened between them; he had wanted it badly. She might not be experienced but no woman could misunderstand the messages his body had given to hers.

To hers?

The sharp sound of Sophia's indrawn breath with its raw note of pain had Ash frowning, his voice harsh as he demanded, 'What's wrong?' Their lovemaking had been intense and passionate and she had given herself fiercely over to it; if he had accidentally caused her discomfort, that was the last thing he had wanted to happen.

'Do you really need to ask?' Sophia challenged him. 'It wasn't me you took to bed tonight, was it, Ash? It was Nasreen. That's my fault for wearing her clothes. I don't know why I did that. It was wrong. I know you still love her.'

Sophia thought he would do something like that? She thought that he could have the kind of powerful, all-consuming sex they had just had and want anyone but her in his arms? Something—a force, a need, a tidal wave of something he could not suppress—rose up inside him.

'No,' he told her. 'I do not still love Nasreen.'

He paused as though his words had somehow caused a seismic movement within himself over which he had no control, and which had now set in motion an unstoppable force within him—a shift in the weight of his burden and its pressure on the dam behind which he had sealed it away. Like an unstoppable landslide it plunged down on that dam, smashing it apart, tearing at its foundations, words he had never expected to hear himself utter in the privacy of his own thoughts, never mind to anyone else, bursting past its barriers in an unchecked torrent, dragged from the depths by the sheer force of the reaction Sophia's accusation had aroused within him.

'The truth is that I never loved Nasreen.'

Shock, disbelief, confusion—Sophia felt them all, but on some deeper level and with the new maturity the short weeks of their marriage had brought her, she could hear the starkness of the truth in Ash's voice. Those words were dragged from him against his wish or control, the first time she had ever seen any break in that control when it came to his silence on the subject of his first wife. The first time he had allowed her to see what lay behind that silence, and what she could see was a man in torment.

Now that he had started to speak, to his own shock Ash discovered that he couldn't stop, the words tumbling from him one after the other, as though desperate to finally be heard.

'I should have loved her. It was my duty to love her.'
His voice was raw with the burden of past pain. 'It was
my duty to make our marriage as filled with love for
each other as my great-grandparents' marriage was.
As a boy growing up, orphaned, with only my nurse's
stories of that love to show me what adult love could
be, I believed that it was enough for me merely to want
to love my chosen bride. I was both naive and arrogant.
I made promises to myself for our marriage that I was
unable to keep. Over the course of our wedding celebra-
tions when I looked at my bride, despite her undoubted
beauty, despite the fact that our marriage was one arranged for us with our best interests at heart, when I
listened to her, when I saw how different our goals in
life were, when I dismissed her as shallow and empty-
headed, selfish and greedy, unkind to those who served
her, and not worthy of the great love I had promised myself I would have for her, I showed that I was the one
who was not worthy, not worthy of my duty, not worthy
of the gift of love shared by my great-grandparents.'

The words were pouring from him with an uncon-
trollable force now, increasingly desperate to escape
and be heard, desperate to escape his desire to have
them silenced, as though a part of him had yearned for
this escape, this stripping down of himself to the bare
bones at the root of his angry contempt for himself, so
that his failings could finally be seen in the clear light
of day. As though somehow he had been waiting for this
moment and this one woman to lay bare his dreadful
weakness and shame, because only she would understand, because only she…

'I should never have married her.'

'You had no choice,' Sophia felt bound to point out.

'I had the choice of choosing another path once I realised that my original goals for our marriage were not achievable. I could and should have chosen then to forge our marriage along different lines, practical royal lines.'

Like their marriage, he meant, Sophia thought. That pain inside her meant nothing. She was as resolved to make their practical marriage work as he was. In fact, she preferred not loving him because not loving him meant that she could not suffer the pain of not being loved back.

'I didn't do that, though. I allowed myself to be directed by my own emotions, by my anger at myself for all that our marriage could never be instead of focusing on what it could be.

'Nasreen was far more practical in that regard. She told me on our wedding night that for her our marriage was merely a diplomatic dynastic union and that her heart along with her body had been given forever to another man.'

Ash heard the shocked indrawn gasp of Sophia's breath.

'She told you that she loved someone else?'

'You pity me? There is no need. The truth is that I was relieved to discover that I would not have to bear the burden of a love from her that I already knew I could not return. However, since I was not prepared to countenance a continuation of their relationship and Nasreen was equally determined that it would continue despite the fact that he was married, there were frequent quarrels and much ill feeling between us. Nasreen's plan for her married life was that she would live the life of a wealthy titled young woman in Mumbai, socialising with her friends. I, on the other hand, wanted her to spend more time here in Nailpur as my maharani, helping me to improve the quality of the lives of my people.

'The night she died we had quarrelled even more than usual. I had gone to Mumbai and brought her back with me against her will to attend a formal court event. I had even insisted that she wear a sari that had been embroidered for her by some of the tribeswomen as a wedding gift.

'Nasreen had objected to all of this. She had further told me that she had no intention of conceiving a child any time soon because being pregnant would stop her from living the life she wanted to live, and that I would have to wait until she was ready.

'I was furious with her, and told her that I would not allow her to return to Mumbai. Whilst I was engaged in a business meeting she left the palace in the sports car she insisted on keeping here because she said that driving it was the only freedom she could have outside of the city. By the time I was alerted to the fact that she had gone, intending to return to Mumbai, it was too late to stop her. And too late to save her.'

Instinctively Sophia reached out towards him in a gesture of sympathy and compassion. How could the touch of such a cool, healing hand on his own burn him with such intense pain? It was his guilt that was responsible for that pain, Ash told himself, that and the knowledge that he did not deserve Sophia's compassion, because he did not deserve anything other than to endure the burden of his terrible guilt. That was the payment he had to make for his arrogance and his pride.

She wasn't hurt by Ash's immediate avoidance of her touch, Sophia assured herself. What she was doing now was simply fulfilling part of her role as his consort. She may not love him as she had done as a teenager, but that did not mean that she could not feel for him, and be touched by this unexpected vulnerability he was showing her.

The promise of the comfort of Sophia's touch had been withdrawn from him. He deserved that loss, Ash berated himself inwardly. He deserved to suffer. He deserved to be punished for setting himself against Nasreen and not finding a way for them to make their marriage work, just because his pride had not been able to tolerate finding any success in their marriage once he had realised he could not love her. He had said too much to Sophia, expressed things he had always sworn to keep to himself, and yet even now, somehow, he could not stop allowing the words he knew damaged him from being said. It was as though he was being driven by a compulsion that wouldn't let him go, a need to reveal to Sophia the very worst of himself in the aftermath of a shared intimacy that had taken him to a place he had never imagined he might find. Because he needed to punish himself for that experience? Because he needed to hear the words out loud to remind himself of exactly what he had done? Ash didn't know. He only knew that he needed to reveal the true horror of what had happened, and that he was culpable.

The deep breath he took tasted acidic in his lungs. Unable to look at Sophia he continued, 'Nasreen must have had the top of the convertible down, because when they found her they discovered that she had been strangled by the scarf of her sari—the sari I insisted she had to wear—as it caught in the wheels of the car.'

Tears burned the backs of Sophia's eyes. Poor

Nasreen and poor Ash, too. What a dreadful, dreadful tragedy. No wonder it had marked Ash so strongly. But Sophia still felt that he was being too hard on himself. That, of course, was typical of the man he was and typical, too, in its way of the younger Ash she remembered, the Ash who believed in doing the right thing and in being honourable, the Ash who had had his idealistic dreams.

'I may not have been able to behave as a man of honour in my duty to love Nasreen,' he continued bleakly, 'but I can and will fulfil my duty to bear my guilt for her death.'

Sophia's heart ached for him. His revelations had shocked her, but more shocking, and far more dangerous, was her awareness of how keenly her own emotions had been touched by his pain.

The danger of that feeling was brought home to her within seconds when Ash told her grimly, 'It was because of my failure to find within myself the love I should have had for Nasreen that this marriage, our marriage, and indeed any second marriage I might have made, is based on practicalities. Emotions are dangerous when they take control of our lives.'

Sophia could agree with that. She knew even now just how dangerous her emotions had been to her when she had loved him so passionately as a girl.

'There is something else I must say. Tonight has again proved to us both, I hope, that we are sexually compatible. That will help to strengthen our marriage. I have also to say how much I appreciate the commitment you are making to my people in your role as maharani. You have an instinctive way with the women and the children. I have watched how they respond to you. It is through you I believe that I will be able to put into effect my plans to improve the education of the poorest amongst the people. I am grateful to you for that, Sophia.'

How truly he was humbling himself, Sophia recognised as she savoured the sweetness of his unexpected praise.

'I am enjoying what I am doing.' It was the truth and she was happy to say so. 'I want to feel that I am making a contribution to the children's future and that I have a useful role to play here in Nailpur, Ash, aside, of course, from that of giving you an heir. Perhaps there is more Santina in me than I ever thought. I don't know. But I do know that my royal role here as your consort is one that I value. The education of the next generation is vitally important and everything I can do to help with that I want to do. I dare say there are plenty of other royal princesses who could have fulfilled the role as well, if not better, than me but—'

'No.' Ash stopped her, cutting across her immediately. 'No. I cannot think of anyone who would make a better maharani than you, Sophia, or who would make a better and more loving mother to our children.'

It was the truth, Ash recognised.

'And there is no one who will make them a more honourable father.' Sophia returned the compliment.

An honourable father, she reflected later, after Ash had left her, but would he be a loving one? Her own father was honourable, but children needed love. There was no doubt that Ash had been badly affected by his marriage to Nasreen, and she could understand why. Remembering the idealistic young man he had been it was easy for her to see how dreadful it would have been for him to be forced to admit that he could not love the bride he had so confidently believed he would love because it was his duty, his destiny, almost, to do so. To have those ideals smashed by his own emotional inability to give Nasreen love would have destroyed the deepest of his core beliefs about himself. She knew how that felt in her own way. She had suffered a terrible loss of sense of self when she had understood the meaning of the gossip about her mother's relationship with the English architect she had admired so much.

But Ash had praised her as his maharani. He had shown her a desire that she could now accept belonged to their relationship. She had responded to that desire; she had welcomed it. These were the foundations on which she must now build her new life, and those foundations would no longer be overshadowed or undermined by her own previous false beliefs about his relationship with Nasreen. There had been a cleansing of that wound, and this was an opportunity for a fresh start between them. Just as long as she remembered and respected the fact that that relationship would be without love.

But that was what she, too, wanted. She didn't want to love Ash all over again and she wasn't going to do so.

CHAPTER NINE

THE sound of Sophia's laughter, warm and spirited, but soft with underlying tenderness, filled the private courtyard she had made her own, and had Ash hurrying towards her, eager to bring her up to date with the results of the soil tests he had just received with a view to enhancing the variety of crops the land could grow. The breaking down of his self-imposed barriers when it came to talking openly to Sophia about his first marriage had brought profound changes to his life, changes which all had their roots in his relationship with Sophia. Maturity had brought a confidence to the natural warmth of her nature, and the courtyard garden had become an oasis to which others seemed naturally drawn when it was occupied by his wife, as they brought her their concerns and their hopes.

As he himself did?

It was only natural that as a husband he should turn to his wife to discuss those issues that affected them both so closely, especially when they were also responsible for the welfare of his people. There was no law that said such discussions had to be held in the solemnity of a grand council chamber rather than discussed in the relaxed atmosphere Sophia had created so skilfully.

As he approached her the sound of the running water of the fountain fell soothingly on his senses, but it was Sophia herself who was responsible for the swift uplift of his heart and the need he felt to smile.

The sound of Sophia's voice had his heart lifting. Because he knew he had made the right decision in marrying her, and because their marriage was working. There was a new atmosphere in the palace. The effects of their shared purposefulness with regard to the people, and the harmony between them, was reflected in the smiles and manner of those who lived close to them. He had much for which to be grateful. He had made the right decision. That decision had been based on logic without emotion just as the passionate intimacy he and Sophia shared in their bed together at night was based on a mutual natural physical desire that was also without the dangerous, potentially damaging effect of emotion. And yet if he was so sure that the decisions he had made were the correct ones, why did he so often feel the sharp sting of anxiety when he thought of Sophia? Why could he not relax until he had heard her laughter and seen her smile with their reassurance for him that she was content with their marriage? Those were emotional reactions after all.

He was simply concerned that she should not overdo things, that was all. She had thrown herself into the new role she had taken on with so much enthusiasm and diligence that it was only natural that he should be concerned.

Sophia tried to still the frantic, giddy, dizzy race of her heartbeat as Ash came towards her. It was just her body's way of reminding her of the pleasure he gave it; it meant nothing else. It happened every time she saw him and she should be used to it by now after these past busy weeks of them working together for the future of his people, even if on this particular occasion there was a legitimate reason for her to feel happy to see him.

She didn't give any indication to him of that, though, when he made an appreciative sound at the sight of the tea tray. She dismissed the maid to pour the tea for him herself, saying with a smile, 'I ordered it when I heard you'd got back from your meeting. How did it go?'

'Even better than I had hoped,' Ash told her, accepting the cup she handed to him. Their fingers touched, Sophia's skin flushing sensually as Ash maintained the contact in a silent promise of the way they would spend the night. The sex between them was a bonus in their marriage that benefited them both, Sophia acknowledged. A bonus which if she was right had already produced a bonus of its own. A happy smile curved her mouth.

'The soil tests have shown that we will be able to grow a much wider variety of crops than even I had hoped for. If all goes well within the next few years the people will not only be self-sufficient in growing their own food, they will also have spare to sell.'

'I'm so pleased, Ash,' Sophia told him truthfully. 'You've worked so hard on this project.'

'No harder than you are working on your projects, Sophia.'

Now was her chance to tell him, Sophia decided. With a relationship like theirs, emotional displays were not the way of things, she knew, but it was impossible for her to keep the small breathless catch out of her voice as she bent her head to tell him meaningfully, 'It seems that we are having the good fortune to progress with all our projects at the moment, Ash, although I cannot be entirely certain until Dr Kumar can confirm my hopes.'

When Ash put down his teacup to look at her, Sophia told him simply, 'I think I'm pregnant.'

She'd known he would be pleased. It was what he'd married her for, after all. But the naked delight and joy that lit up his face caught at her heart, every bit as much as the way he got to his feet and came to her, saying her name in a voice that trembled slightly as he took hold of both her hands in his; it made her heart turn over inside her chest all over again. She had suspected for several days that she could be pregnant. She had known that Ash would be pleased if she was—she had known that she would be delighted herself—but this unexpected and unlooked-for tender act of husbandly intimacy could only be affecting her with such intensity because of the pregnancy hormones that had been released into her system, she assured herself as she battled against the need to cling to him and be held by him, held close in his arms as those arms bound both her and their child to him.

'I shall send for Dr Kumar immediately,' Ash told her. The news Sophia had just given him was so welcome and wanted that that was why he felt the way he did, elated, delighted and yet at the same time anxious for Sophia, proud of her and very, very protective of her. It was because their child was so important that he felt like this. So much of the future depended on them producing an heir, after all.

'It's still very early days,' Sophia felt bound to warn him.

'Then you must be even more careful not to overdo

things. It would be more restful for you if you could cur-
tail your duties here and perhaps go to Mumbai where
you could rest more, but with the rainy season starting
there...'

Ash was pacing the courtyard now, plainly concerned. A small smile softened Sophia's mouth. Wasn't
this the universal reaction of new fathers-to-be to the
creation of that new life they wanted so much and which
they instinctively wanted to protect?

'I have no desire at all to go to Mumbai, Ash,' she
told him. 'I can rest perfectly well here if I need to rest,
which I most certainly do not at the moment. I want
to be here. This is our home and it will be our child's
home, and as for me overdoing things—Ash, I am a
healthy young woman and pregnancy is a perfectly natural function.'

'I don't want you—'

'You don't want me taking any unnecessary risks for
your child. I know that, and I promise you that I shan't,
but you mustn't try to wrap me in cotton wool.'

'I just want—'

'To protect your child.'

To protect *you,* he wanted to say, but Ash knew as
the thought formed that it was not one he was permitted. By his own rules. Rules he had put in place to protect their marriage and now their child.

She was in danger of feeling far too emotional,
Sophia recognised, and that she could not and would
not do. The best way to deal with such a situation as
she was now learning was to concentrate instead on
something practical, something achievable, something
that did not involve her mourning what she could never
have. So she changed the subject to say practically, 'It

was a good idea of yours to suggest that we donate Nasreen's clothes to charity. We've had the most lovely letters from the various charities I contacted saying how grateful they are to receive such a donation in Nasreen's name.'

He didn't want to talk about Nasreen or her clothes or even the charities they were benefiting, Ash thought. He wanted to talk about them, about their child, about their future. But a newly pregnant Sophia must be protected and indulged, he decided, although he was unable to stop himself from pointing out, 'Your idea to create scholarships in her memory was very generous, Sophia. By rights they should be in your name because Nasreen would certainly never have thought of doing anything so generous.'

'I am happy to be generous on her behalf,' Sophia assured him.

The truth was that she wanted peace for Ash more than she wanted to do something for Nasreen, especially now that she was carrying their child. And after all, wasn't it only natural that as that child's mother she wanted him or her to have the full commitment of his or her father without any darkness from the past overshadowing him? What she could not and would never ask Ash for, for her own benefit, she could and would, Sophia was beginning to realise very determinedly, work towards asking for their child. That was the nature of motherhood, was it not?

And the growing longing she was experiencing to feel emotionally closer to Ash, was that only because of her instinctive desire to secure a father's love for her child? Why not? As a child herself she had known what it was to feel she had cause to doubt her father's love for her and she certainly didn't want that for her child. Wasn't it only natural that she should be particularly anxious to ensure that her own child was loved by Ash? It was for their child that she wanted them to be close, not for herself. Ash, she felt, had been too hurt, too damaged, by what he saw as a failure within himself to ever come anywhere near risking breaking the vow he had made to keep their marriage emotion-free for its own safety. She would be a fool to allow herself to pin any dreams on that changing.

And did she want it to change?

The very fact that she couldn't let herself answer her own question was a warning she needed to heed, Sophia told herself.

The gel that had been placed on her tummy by the radiographer in charge of the expensive new scanning equipment in Nailpur's new hospital's maternity wing felt cold, and Sophia gave a small gasp that had Ash looking sharply at her. She had been surprised but pleased when he had insisted on coming with her for her scan, but his protective concern wasn't for her, she reminded herself. It was for their child, his child and heir. Not for her the tenderness of a husband who reached for her hand whilst the scan was in progress, sharing the special magic of the moment with her as it united them emotionally. Instead, Ash was standing slightly to one side of her, so that it was towards him and not her that the radiographer looked when she announced a little breathlessly, 'Highness, the maharani is carrying twins—boy twins.'

There was no logical reason why the scent of Ash's skin, as he leaned across her to look at the images on the screen being pointed out by the radiographer, should fill her with such an intense surge of emotional longing for the right to reach out and take hold of his hand and to have him look at *her* with the same mix of awe and disbelieving male pride in his gaze she could see he had for his sons. But she couldn't deny the fact that it did. This should have been a special moment for them as parents but instead she felt as though she didn't matter as herself, her only value in the room that was now rapidly filling up with medical personnel including the royal physician was as that of the woman who was carrying Nailpur's precious heirs.

It made no difference either telling herself that she not only should have expected this but that as a royal princess in a convenient marriage she should also have been prepared for it. Her heart bumped heavily into her ribs. She was delighted to be pregnant, of course she was, but she also felt very alone just at a time when surely she most needed to feel valued and… And what? Cherished? Adored? *Loved?*

Her heart thumped again but no one else in the room including Ash himself seemed to notice or care. If only Ash would just look at her, just share this special time with her in some small private way, it would make all the difference, but instead he had his back to her as he talked with Dr Kumar. Could a man who could ignore his wife at such a special time give the sons he was so proud of creating right now the love that they would need, a true father's love? The kind of love she herself had craved and been denied by her own father? Was it natural for a woman who had every reason to be on top of the world to feel so vulnerable and anxious, instead?

Ash didn't dare allow himself to look at Sophia. That

feeling he had of wanting to reach out to her and take hold of her hand instead of having to stand by and simply watch as the radiographer prepared her for the scan had unsettled him. It ran so counter to everything he expected from himself with regard to their relationship. It spoke of feelings he had no right to have. And then if that hadn't been enough for him to have to deal with, there was his reaction to the news that they were to have twin sons. The surge of joy he had felt was natural and allowable. A man in his position would naturally feel such joy after all, but that other feeling...that surge of protective anxiety for Sophia herself? That was because he was concerned for her as the mother of his sons, that was all.

The medical staff were finally turning towards her, all beaming faces and delight for her, although it was to Ash that they spoke in answer to his brusque question about the risks attached to a twin pregnancy, as they reassured him that there was no cause for any concern, and that both babies were of similar, healthy weight and measurements.

On the face of it they could have been any couple confronted with the news that where they had expected confirmation of the conception of one child they were now having the double pleasure and excitement of realising that there were going to be two, Sophia acknowledged. She tried determinedly not to allow her own feelings of vulnerability to spoil what she wanted to be a happy moment for them both, even if she had to accept that it wasn't going to be a moment that united them as a couple, as well as parents-to-be. It was just an upsurge of pregnancy hormones that was making her feel so vulnerable and so in need of Ash's emotional support, a clever device invented by mother nature to ensure that a pregnant woman did everything she could to keep the father of the child she was carrying as close to her as she could. After all, in prehistoric times the survival of both her and her child would have depended on the willingness and the ability of the father to keep them safe and fed. It made her feel better to be able to give herself this rational explanation for feelings that had made her feel so vulnerable. And it stopped her wanting that physical and emotional closeness to Ash that had so caught her off guard, didn't it?

She had her babies to think about now, not just herself. She was still learning what it meant to be Ash's wife and to live by the rules he had imposed on their marriage, and the truth was that living by those rules didn't come naturally or easily to someone who had always wanted to marry for love. Motherhood, on the other hand, and her feelings of maternal love and protection for the babies she was carrying, was as instinctive and as natural to her as breathing. Just like wanting to reach for Ash's hand when she had had her scan. But that was forbidden.

How many other things would be forbidden under the complex barriers Ash had erected against love? Would those barriers come between him and his sons? Would they, too, be denied emotional intimacy with their father? Sophia gave a small shiver despite the sunny warmth of the airy room. She must not look for problems. She must be positive and she must be strong—for the sake of their babies.

'There is no doubt that your people will welcome the arrival of your sons, Highness,' the royal physician was saying.

Sons. Another unexpected pang gouged Sophia's sensitive emotions. Had she been carrying daughters, how much of a solace might they have been to her as they grew up, members of her own sex with whom she might have had a special closeness that helped to alleviate the loneliness of being an unloved wife. Sons would be raised as future leaders of their people; sons would align themselves to their father. Sons would pattern themselves on that father. Another chill of dread shivered over her body. That wasn't what she wanted for her sons. She wanted them to grow up knowing what love was and valuing it.

'It is a gift indeed that there should be two children, for us and for them,' said Ash to Dr Kumar.

Sophia was so delicately built despite her lush curves. The thought of her carrying two babies was causing Ash anxieties for which he hadn't been prepared. Of course, it was only natural that he should be concerned for her well-being. He knew all about the loneliness suffered by a child who lost a parent, and it was equally natural therefore that there should be that core of anxiety within him for Sophia's health and safe delivery.

Suddenly, as pleased as he was about the conception of his sons, Ash was also aware of a need to withdraw into himself so that he could put a safe distance between himself and the dangerous intensity of the emotions that were threatening to take control of him.

'I have to go,' Ash told Sophia abruptly, still not looking directly at her. 'I have a meeting I have to attend. Dr Kumar will arrange for you to be driven back to the palace and I shall have a word with him about having a nurse on hand there—'

'No. That's ridiculous and unnecessary.' Sophia

stopped him, whilst the medical staff discreetly disappeared, leaving them alone in the room.

'I'm not sick, Ash, I'm pregnant—and healthily pregnant, too.'

'You are—'

'—carrying your heirs, yes, I know, and I hope that you don't think that I would do anything that would prejudice me carrying them safely to full term.'

Sophia's feisty reaction warned Ash that she wasn't going to allow him to wrap her in cotton wool.

'I simply want to make sure that all three of you receive the best care possible,' Ash defended himself.

All three of them, when he hadn't even cared enough about her to understand how much she had needed some small show of physical affection from him earlier on whilst she had waited to see her scan?

She must not allow herself to become downhearted, Sophia warned herself later as she was driven back to the palace. It had been a shock for both of them to discover that she was carrying twins. Surely the knowledge that they were to become parents was bound to bring them closer? After all, it was what they both wanted.

CHAPTER TEN

IT WAS almost exactly a month since her scan, but far from bringing them closer together those four weeks had, if anything, led to Ash putting an even greater distance between them, Sophia thought as she sat alone in her private courtyard garden in the welcome cool of the evening.

Where the twins were concerned, Ash was scrupulous about keeping a check on their health and her own, but whenever she tried to talk to him on any kind of personal level he retreated from her and changed the subject.

And most humiliating of all for her, as her own need and indeed craving for a loving gentle intimacy with him grew, along with her feelings of emotional insecurity, Ash had rejected her by no longer coming to her bed.

Whilst part of her—the old feisty Sophia—longed to demand to know what had happened to the sexual chemistry he had told her existed between them, the new mother-in-waiting Sophia was far too protective of the future emotional security of the babies she was carrying to want to risk a confrontation that could destroy the increasingly fragile bonds that held them together.

Besides, she seriously thought that Ash's distance from her was the way things were going to be and that nothing she could say or do could change that, and that really scared her. Not for her own sake but for the sake of their sons. It was one thing for Ash to refuse to let her get close to him, but increasingly she was worrying that he might behave in exactly the same way with the twins, locking them out emotionally. Not necessarily deliberately—she knew how pleased he was about them—but because he simply couldn't help himself?

She had grown up with a distant father whom she had felt had rejected every attempt she had made to get close to him. She couldn't bear the thought of that happening to her precious babies. But they would have her, and Ash would be a good and protective father in many other ways. Right now, because her pregnancy was making her feel so emotionally vulnerable, she was achingly conscious of all that she was missing as a woman by not having a husband who loved her, but it was the twins who mattered most, not her. There was no sacrifice of her own personal happiness she was not prepared to make to give them the security of growing up with their parents living together. That didn't mean that she wasn't right to feel concerned that Ash might not be able to stop his attitude towards her from spilling over into his behaviour towards his sons.

In the privacy of his own suite, Ash paced the floor of his office. He had taken to working late into the evening, telling himself that he needed to ensure that all his projects were up to date ahead of the birth of the twins, but he knew that the reality was he worked late because that was the only way he had of blotting out the demons that were stalking him.

It was illogical and…and *unnecessary, unwanted and unacceptable* to him, this almost constant need he had to be with Sophia. And not just to be with her. He wanted… Ash stopped pacing, a dark frown slashing his forehead. He had told himself that it would be no hardship for a man of his level of self-discipline to deny himself Sophia's bed as a precautionary measure to ensure the safety of her pregnancy—after all, as good and passionate as the sex between them had been it was only sex—but the truth was that with every night without her, his desire for her found a thousand different new ways in which to torture him. Just the memory of the scent of her skin, the sound of her breath as it accelerated with the desire he had stoked, the small mewling sounds of increasingly out-of-control pleasure she made when he aroused her, all of those just by themselves were enough to have a need coursing through him that left him feeling as though he had been burned with acid and left raw and close to crying out with the pain of his wounds.

He had lost count of the number of times he had woken in the night thinking he could hear her breathing, conjuring up out of the darkness the sound of her voice as she whispered his name so sweetly when she pleaded with him not just for the pleasure he gave her but also for the right to return that pleasure to him. How could one single woman in the space of a handful of weeks have come to have such a powerful effect on him? He had desired women before. But never as much as he desired Sophia, and certainly never as much as he needed the sweet agony the desire gave him.

That he should feel like this was a warning to him, Ash told himself. A warning and a test. He must surely prove to himself that he could stay away from Sophia's bed—in the first instance for the practical reason of not wanting to endanger her pregnancy in any way, especially as she was carrying twins, but in the second instance so that by the time they were sharing a bed again the need he felt for her would be under his control, not the other way around.

Given all that, why was he right now walking down the corridor that led to Sophia's room?

She knew it wasn't the sensible thing to do. Surely she'd spent far too many hours preparing herself logically for what her life with Ash was going to be like to waste all that effort on some kind of irrational emotional outburst, or even worse, the kind of emotionally demanding behaviour that was bound to make Ash retreat even further from her?

This wasn't about her, Sophia reminded herself as she hurried towards her bedroom door, intent on seeking Ash out to confront him with her growing concern about how his emotional distance from her could impact on their sons if he behaved the same way towards them. She'd been on her way to bed when the emotional firestorm that was now propelling her towards her bedroom door had struck, leaving her to pull a robe on over her cobweb-fine silk nightgown.

Ash reached out for the handle to Sophia's bedroom door. He should not be doing this. An ice-cold river of self-loathing held him immobile whilst also trapping his emotions in its familiar numbing wasteland. Even his heartbeat seemed to have slowed in tune with the emptiness that had now filled the gap left by the rush of longing that had brought him here. His hand fell back to his side just as inside the bedroom Sophia pulled open the door.

The unexpectedness of seeing Ash there, outside her bedroom door, obviously on his way to see her—where else could he be going, after all?—flooded her with so much happiness that she immediately reached out to him, her hand on his arm as she urged him inside her room, her joy showing in the warmth in her voice as she said his name.

Automatically Ash allowed himself to be drawn towards her. Her open delight at seeing him was confusing the ice-cold deadening river of controlled self-loathing inside him. His gaze—the one that only seconds ago under the influence of that deadening flow had, like his other senses, assured him that there was nothing about any aspect of Sophia that could break through the barriers he had so regrettably allowed to weaken in the privacy of his own treacherous thoughts—could see the sweet warmth of the curve of her lips, lips which he already knew were so soft and incredibly responsive to his kisses that just to look at them was enough to have them quivering with longing, and her body softening with desire for him just as right now his was hardening with its desire for her.

He must not think about that. He dragged his gaze from her face and then realised his mistake as it slipped to her body, its burgeoning shape revealed to him through the flimsiness of the nightgown he could see beneath her open robe. Her breasts looked fuller, her belly rounding. His heartbeat had picked up and was now racing, thumping, in fact, with the renewed force of his longing to reach out for her and take hold of her, to discover her newly forming body with his fingertips so that he could learn its promise and rejoice in the gift it was holding.

Ash was here. She had been allowing her silly vulnerability to get the better of her. He was here and soon he would hold her and in the secret darkness of their bed they would share an intimacy that surely she could build on to sustain her. Only now that he was here could she admit to herself the true depth of the sense of loss and abandonment she had felt through his absence from her bed. In fact, she was physically trembling with the intensity of her relief—trembling inside and close to tears caused by that relief, as well. Perhaps there was hope for the future after all. It was obvious that she had misjudged the situation in thinking that Ash didn't want her any more now that she was pregnant. Loving him meant...

Loving him? Loving Ash? Her heart felt as though it had been thrown into a theme park ride and was now racing upward towards the final terrifying drop. When had love crept into the equation? It wasn't a question Sophia was in any state of mind to answer. All she did know was that in one blinding moment of clarity she had been shown the reality of her own feelings. She loved Ash. Hadn't she read somewhere that women were engineered differently than men by nature, to produce a hormone during sex that automatically forged a unique bond by that woman's senses and emotions to the man with whom she had shared the experience?

And wasn't it the truth that she had already been programmed to love Ash by her own past even if she had genuinely believed that he had killed that teenage adoration with his rejection of her?

Love. For her husband and their sons. Surely that was something worth fighting for, something worth striving and hoping for? They were already married, and...

And Ash had sworn never to allow himself to look for love within their marriage.

But he was here. He had come to her.

Here in this room was everything in his world that held real value, Ash found himself thinking. Here was everything he could ever want or need because here was Sophia.

He moved closer to her just as she moved closer to him, an appeal in her eyes that he couldn't misunderstand. His body certainly wasn't misunderstanding it. His body was welcoming that soft look of female need she was giving him.

'Ash.' All Sophia's pent-up emotion trembled through her voice. Ash was so close to her. He was within touching distance of her.

'Ash.' She whispered his name this time, and then felt the warm gust of his breath against her lips as he exhaled in response before bending his head to kiss her.

He wanted her so much. His body was on fire with that need. It had already gone far too long without her, and it hungered for her. As though something inside him had snapped Ash felt his self-control break. Wrapping Sophia in his arms he began to kiss her over and over again, the sensuality of his passion turning her weak with her own response to it as she returned each increasingly deep kiss.

Unable to stop himself, Ash started to caress Sophia's body, the full curves of her breasts with their dark crests so clearly visible beneath the fine silk and so responsive to his touch, causing her to make small sounds of pleasure deep down in her throat. Her head was thrown back against his supporting arm as he brought those sweet moans of pleasure from her. He couldn't wait to take her to bed and complete their lovemaking. His body ached and burned for that intimacy and that release; it dragged out the need racking him so that he could feel it in every nerve ending. He kissed her hungrily, savouring the sweet rich taste of her, the pleasure that lay within the warmth of her mouth, his free hand automatically moving lower over her body and then stilling when it encountered the soft swell of her pregnancy.

Lost beneath the intensity of Ash's kiss and her own response to it, at first Sophia couldn't quite take in what was happening when Ash abruptly stopped kissing her and pushed her away from him, releasing her.

'What is it?' she asked him shakily. 'What's wrong?'

'The twins,' was all Ash could bring himself to say, his voice terse as he half turned away from her to conceal from her his own disgust with himself. How could he have been so lost to all sense of what it meant to be a father to have allowed his desire to drive him towards an action that might have endangered the twins' safety and Sophia's physical comfort? He was disgusted with himself.

'The twins?' was all Sophia could manage to repeat as she tried to cling to the remnants of her dignity, pulling it around herself in much the same way in which she was now drawing her open robe around her body.

After the realisation that she loved Ash, his appearance in her bedroom and then her hopes heightened by what had looked as though it was going to turn into intense lovemaking, his rejection of her now was unbearably painful.

'I don't want…' Ash began, but Sophia was in no mood to let him continue. Where there had been hope and arousal, there was now disappointment, hurt and anger—the hurt anger of a feisty woman who wanted her man but who was being rejected by him.

'You don't want me any more now that I'm pregnant, is that what you were going to say? I'm carrying your sons so you don't have to have sex with me any more, is that it? What about that sexual chemistry between us you spoke of when you were persuading me to marry you, Ash, or did that only exist when you were thinking about me conceiving your heir? Or maybe it's just that you don't find me desirable now that I'm pregnant. But whatever the case, I want you to know that coming here and…and…and doing what you did and then rejecting me isn't the kind of behaviour I expect from a man like you. It's…it's cruel and…and unfair.' Her voice was becoming thick with the tears she was determined not to unleash. Ash was standing with his face averted from her, and not moving at all.

He was ignoring her, blocking her out, distancing himself from her. Because he didn't want her in his life at all, really? Because he never had and he never would?

It was too much for her to endure.

'Did you ever really desire me at all, Ash, or was it just something you forced yourself to pretend?'

'No.' The denial was ripped from Ash's throat before he could silence it, the sheer intensity of the emotions inside him that had broken through physically forcing him to turn round, and look at Sophia. 'Of course I wanted you.' He wanted her now. He wanted to go to her and take hold of her and show her how wrong she was, but he had her to think of, and the twins. He was a husband and a father-to-be now and not just a man burning and driven by his own shameful lusts.

'But you haven't been near me for weeks, and just now...'

'I was thinking of the twins and of you. I didn't want...' It was so hard for him to admit to any kind of emotional vulnerability but his moral need to set the record straight was stronger than his need to protect his defences.

'I didn't want to risk hurting them or...or you. You are so small and you are carrying two babies.'

There was a huge lump in Sophia's throat. She couldn't deny the truth she could hear in Ash's voice. She couldn't argue against such an obviously genuine explanation. But why couldn't he have told her that before?

'I'm a woman, Ash. I'm designed by nature to carry your sons safely. And women do have sex when they're pregnant, you know.'

'I didn't want to take any unnecessary risks.'

Yes, she understood his fears. But why couldn't he have opened up to her and explained what was in his thoughts? He couldn't because Ash didn't deal in emotions.

The warmth she had felt when he had explained why he had stayed away from her had turned to the cold chill of a returning fear that was already worrying her, namely that Ash would not be able to relate emotionally to his sons and that he would keep them at a distance, because he no longer knew how to relate emotionally to others.

Ash saw the pain darkening Sophia's eyes and the sadness shadowing her face. 'What is it? What's wrong?' he asked her.

'I know how much the twins mean to you, Ash, but I'm worried that *they'll* never know, because you will never be able to show them or tell them how much they mean to you. I'm afraid that you'll distance yourself from them in the same way that you distance yourself from me. I know how much that hurts, having a father who doesn't seem to care. That kind of thing can hurt a child so very badly and make them feel so rejected. A child can't rationalise that it might just be that a father does care but can't show those feelings. I want our sons to know the real Ash, the Ash that I knew whilst I was growing up, the kind, understanding, always ready to listen, happy Ash whom I loved so much. I want you to be that Ash for our children, but I'm afraid that they will never know him, because the Ash you feel you have to be now has locked him away and will never let him be free to enjoy his children and to love them.'

Every emotion-filled, spoken-from-the-heart word Sophia offered felt a like a seismic shock deep inside Ash that shook him to the core. He knew with a flash of insight and at the most powerful deepest intense level of himself that Sophia's words had touched a nerve, set in motion a reaction like the clicking open of a series of locks that had opened doors inside him that showed him an inescapable truth. That truth was that he couldn't bear to be the man Sophia had just described to him, the man who whilst loving his children could not reach out to them and so left them to feel that he didn't care, and the husband who wanted and needed his wife so much that he was filled with fear because of those feelings.

'Sophia!' Her name broke from his heart and tore at his lungs, his stride towards her to reach her swift and slightly uncoordinated, his breathing unsteady. A fine tremor gripped his body as he held her hands in his own and told her thickly, 'I promise you that I will be the father you want me to be for our sons, that I will try to be the Ash you remember for them and that they will never, ever have to doubt my love for them.'

'Oh, Ash.'

'And as for me not wanting you…'

He was kissing her so sweetly and tenderly, drawing her close to his body so that she could feel for herself his desire for her, that it was impossible for Sophia not to respond.

'I don't want to hurt you or the babies,' Ash was whispering to her in a voice raw with a desire he wasn't making any attempt to hide.

'You won't,' Sophia assured him. 'We can be careful and make it slow and sweet, and…'

The violent shudder that racked Ash's body told her more than any words how much hers had affected him. But when he carried her to the bed and then carefully undressed her to gaze reverentially at her naked body, it was her turn to tremble with the intensity of her emotions.

Had she really thought that Ash might be turned off by the changes in her body? If so he was showing her now just how wrong she had been, with the warmth of the long, slow, deep kiss he was giving her.

All the new sweetness of the lives they had created together and the love she had now discovered for him were in Sophia's response to Ash. Her lips clung to his, her arms reaching out to hold him, her heart melting with the tide of feeling that swept through her when Ash placed his hand on the rounding shape of her body. There was something so inexpressibly tender and special about such a touch, about the contact between father and child, and the warmth of his caress on her own skin at the same time conveying to her body a sense of care and protection.

But it wasn't just care and protection she wanted from Ash. Her body ached with a hot but gentle sweetness for him and for his lovemaking. And as though he knew exactly how she felt and exactly what she needed and longed for, it seemed somehow to Sophia that with every touch and caress Ash brought a new and deeper meaning to their lovemaking, as though he *wanted* to bring a new and a deeper meaning to that lovemaking.

The kisses he placed on her belly, the sweet slowness of his possession of her as he waited for her to reassure him that she wanted that possession, spoke so clearly of a man who genuinely cared not just for the welfare of his children but for her, as well. And when the final moment of her pleasure came it brought with it for Sophia an upsurge of emotional tears. She loved him so much.

Feeling Sophia's tears dampen his face Ash's first reaction was one of concern that he had, despite the care he had taken, still managed to hurt her, and the shake of her head which she gave in answer to his question had him demanding urgently, 'Then what is it?'

'I'm afraid, Ash,' Sophia admitted, the intimacy of their entwined bodies, the tenderness of the moment and her love for him overwhelming her natural instinct to conceal her feelings from him. 'You see, I've fallen in love with you all over again, and sometimes I just don't know how I'm going to be able to cope with that when I know that you don't want my love.'

Later Ash would remember this second out of time and believe that he had actually physically felt the cracking apart of the wall he had built around his emotions, but right now it was the splashing down of one single tear and then another from his own eyes onto Sophia's damp face that told him all he needed to know. He, who had never been able to cry for any of his own pain or grief, was weeping now for the pain he had caused Sophia, because he loved her, because her pain was worse for him to bear than his own could ever be, and he was the one who had caused that pain.

'I do want your love, Sophia,' he told her. 'I want it and you more than I have ever or could ever want anything or anyone else in my life. I've known that for weeks, although I've been trying to deny it. You say that you are afraid. I have been afraid, too, afraid to admit how much you mean to me, so very afraid that I couldn't even allow myself to admit to that fear. It was easier to pretend that it wasn't happening. Easier to make rules for you to obey than to risk admitting that no rules on earth can overpower true love. I've known what's been happening to me but I've still tried to fight it, to push you away, to punish myself for even thinking about how I feel about you.'

'You really mean it?' Sophia asked him tremulously. 'You really do love me?'

To see his feisty, brave-hearted Sophia so vulnerable because of his cowardice tore at Ash's heart. 'Yes. I really do and I really mean it. I intend to spend the rest of my life proving to you just how precious you are to me. You'll need to help me though, Sophia. I'll make mistakes, and get things wrong. I'll need you to show me how to love you and the babies in the way you deserve to be loved. You'll have to teach me through your own sweet, loving, generous example.'

'I will. I'll show you every day, my darling, darling Ash,' Sophia assured him tenderly as she cupped the side of his face with her hand and kissed him softly.

Tears for her, fallen from the eyes of the man who loved her, had washed the last of the doubt from her heart.

A tiny flutter of movement, followed by another inside her body, had her giving a small gasp and immediately reaching for Ash's hand to place it over her stomach.

'It's your sons, letting us know that they definitely approve of two parents who love each other,' she told Ash. And when he bent his head and kissed first on the place where his hand had been and then cupped her face to kiss her, Sophia knew that when it came to learning how to show his love for them, her husband was going to be a very good pupil, indeed.

EPILOGUE

It was no good, Sophia admitted. Although she'd wanted to have a natural delivery, she'd had to give in, not so much because Dr Kumar and the obstetrician brought in by him from Mumbai had insisted that a planned C-section was the safest way to deliver the twins now that they were getting so big, but because of the very real fear she'd seen in Ash's eyes.

He'd told her that it must be her choice but she'd seen how worried he was, and last night after the medical team had delivered its verdict, she'd woken up to find Ash pacing the floor of the bedroom they now shared, and he'd admitted to her how terrified he was that he might lose her.

'Nasreen died because I didn't care. I'm so afraid that I might lose you because I care so very much.'

He hadn't added 'as a punishment,' but Sophia had known that was what he meant, and immediately she'd known that she couldn't let him suffer the anxiety of her going through a natural birth.

So now here she was at the hospital, and Ash was pacing the floor nervously once again, as the medical personnel went about the business of preparing her for the delivery of their sons.

'It really is the most sensible option,' the obstetrician told her. 'You've got over three weeks to go to your natural delivery date and the twins are so big already that I just would not be happy about that, for their sake, as well as your own.'

Sophia nodded her head, and reached for Ash's hand as he came to stand at her side.

'I love you so much,' he whispered to her, and Sophia felt his hand tighten on hers as the operation began, and first one and then the second of their sons was lifted from Sophia's body and handed to their parents.

For Sophia, seeing the look on Ash's face as he held one and then the other of their babies before giving them to her to hold told her beyond the need for any words just how much love their sons would have from their father. They would bond and form a male trio that at times as the twins grew would exclude her, as a woman, but the bond that she and Ash shared would be so strong that it would hold them together for ever, through the birth of other children hopefully, during the growing up of those children and into those years when they would perhaps become grandparents. A bond of the truest kind of love, given from the heart of a man who'd had to overcome so much to be able to make that gift.

'I promise you I will be the father you want for them, Sophia,' Ash told her tenderly. 'And the loving husband that you so deserve.'

* * * * *

CLASSIC

Harlequin *Presents*

REQUEST YOUR FREE BOOKS!

◆ Harlequin *Presents*

PASSION · GUARANTEED · SEDUCTION

2 FREE NOVELS PLUS
2 FREE GIFTS!

YES! Please send me 2 FREE Harlequin Presents® novels and my 2 FREE gifts (gifts are worth about $10). After receiving them, if I don't wish to receive any more books, I can return the shipping statement marked "cancel." If I don't cancel, I will receive 6 brand-new novels every month and be billed just $4.30 per book in the U.S. or $4.99 per book in Canada. That's a saving of at least 14% off the cover price! It's quite a bargain! Shipping and handling is just 50¢ per book in the U.S. and 75¢ per book in Canada.* I understand that accepting the 2 free books and gifts places me under no obligation to buy anything. I can always return a shipment and cancel at any time. Even if I never buy another book, the two free books and gifts are mine to keep forever.   106/306 HDN FERQ

Name _____ (PLEASE PRINT)

Address _____ Apt. #

City _____ State/Prov. _____ Zip/Postal Code

Signature (if under 18, a parent or guardian must sign)

Mail to the **Reader Service:**
IN U.S.A.: P.O. Box 1867, Buffalo, NY 14240-1867
IN CANADA: P.O. Box 609, Fort Erie, Ontario L2A 5X3

Not valid for current subscribers to Harlequin Presents books.

**Are you a current subscriber to Harlequin Presents books
and want to receive the larger-print edition?
Call 1-800-873-8635 or visit www.ReaderService.com.**

* Terms and prices subject to change without notice. Prices do not include applicable taxes. Sales tax applicable in N.Y. Canadian residents will be charged applicable taxes. Offer not valid in Quebec. This offer is limited to one order per household. All orders subject to credit approval. Credit or debit balances in a customer's account(s) may be offset by any other outstanding balance owed by or to the customer. Please allow 4 to 6 weeks for delivery. Offer available while quantities last.

Your Privacy—The Reader Service is committed to protecting your privacy. Our Privacy Policy is available online at www.ReaderService.com or upon request from the Reader Service.

We make a portion of our mailing list available to reputable third parties that offer products we believe may interest you. If you prefer that we not exchange your name with third parties, or if you wish to clarify or modify your communication preferences, please visit us at www.ReaderService.com/consumerschoice or write to us at Reader Service Preference Service, P.O. Box 9062, Buffalo, NY 14269. Include your complete name and address.

HP11B

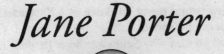

The legacy of the powerful
Sicilian Ferrara dynasty continues in
THE FORBIDDEN FERRARA
by USA TODAY *bestselling author Sarah Morgan.*

Enjoy this sneak peek!

A Ferrara would never sit down at a Baracchi table for fear of being poisoned.

Fia had no idea why Santo was here. He didn't know.

He *couldn't* know.

"*Buona sera,* Fia."

A deep male voice came from the doorway, and she turned. The crazy thing was, she didn't know his voice. But she knew his eyes and they were looking at her now—two dark pools of dangerous black. They gleamed bright with intelligence and hard with ruthless purpose. They were the eyes of a man who thrived in a cutthroat business environment. A man who knew what he wanted and wasn't afraid to go after it. They were the same eyes that had glittered into hers in the darkness three years before as they'd ripped each other's clothes and slaked a fierce hunger.

He was exactly the same. Still the same "born to rule" Ferrara self-confidence; the same innate sophistication, polished until it shone bright as the paintwork of his Lamborghini.

She wanted him to go to hell and stay there.

He was her biggest mistake.

And judging from the cold, cynical glint in his eye, he considered her to be his.

"Well, this is a surprise. The Ferrara brothers don't usually step down from their ivory tower to mingle with us mortals. Checking out the competition?" She adopted her

EXP0612

most businesslike tone, while all the time her anxiety was rising and the questions were pounding through her head.

Did he know?

Had he found out?

A faint smile touched his mouth and the movement distracted her. There was an almost deadly beauty in the sensual curve of those lips. Everything about the man was dark and sexual, as if he'd been designed for the express purpose of drawing women to their doom. If rumor were correct, he did that with appalling frequency.

Fia wasn't fooled by his apparently relaxed pose or his deceptively mild tone.

Santo Ferrara was the most dangerous man she'd ever met.

Will Santo discover Fia's secret?

Find out in THE FORBIDDEN FERRARA
by USA TODAY bestselling author Sarah Morgan,
available this June from Harlequin Presents®!

Harlequin *Romance*

A touching new duet from fan-favorite author

SUSAN MEIER

First Time **DADS!**

When millionaire CEO Max Montgomery spots
Kate Hunter-Montgomery—the wife he's never forgotten—
back in town with a daughter who looks just like him, he's
determined to win her back. But can this savvy business tycoon
convince Kate to trust him a second time with her heart?

Find out this June in

THE TYCOON'S SECRET DAUGHTER

And look for book 2 coming this August!

NANNY FOR THE MILLIONAIRE'S TWINS

Saddle up with Harlequin® series books this summer
and find a cowboy for every mood!

SPECIAL EDITION

Life, Love and Family

USA TODAY bestselling author

Marie Ferrarella

enchants readers in

ONCE UPON A MATCHMAKER

Micah Muldare's aunt is worried that her nephew is going to wind up alone in his old age...but this matchmaking mama has just the thing! When Micah finds himself accused of theft, defense lawyer Tracy Ryan agrees to help him as a favor to his aunt, but soon finds herself drawn to more than just his case. Will Micah open up his heart and realize Tracy is his match?

Available June 2012

Saddle up with Harlequin® series books this summer and find a cowboy for every mood!

Available wherever books are sold.